BAR HARBOR

A SHORT STORY COLLECTION

ALSO BY

J.B. HOGAN

TIN HOLLOW

FALLEN: A SHORT STORY COLLECTION

THE RUBICON: POETRY & SHORT FICTION

MEXICAN SKIES

TIME AFTER TIME: THE CURIOUS CASE OF MR. STEPHEN WHITE

LOSING COTTON

LIVING BEHIND TIME

BAR HARBOR

A SHORT STORY COLLECTION

J.B. HOGAN

AUTHOR OF FALLEN

LIFFEY
PRESS

an imprint of
THE OGHMA PRESS

OGHMA

C R E A T I V E   M E D I A

Liffey Press
An imprint of Oghma Creative Media, Inc.
2401 Beth Lane, Bentonville, Arkansas 72712

Library of Congress Cataloging-in-Publication Data

Names: Hogan, J.B., author.
Title: Bar Harbor/J.B. Hogan.
Description: First Edition | Bentonville: Liffey, 2022
Identifiers: LCCN: 2020935340 | ISBN: 978-1-63373-581-1(hardcover) |
ISBN: 978-1-63373-582-8 (trade paperback) | ISBN: 978-1-63373-583-5 (eBook)
Subjects: | BISAC: FICTION/Short Stories (single author) | FICTION/Literary |
LC record available at: https://lccn.loc.gov/2020935340

Liffey Press trade paperback edition July, 2022

Cover & Interior Design by Casey W. Cowan
Editing by Gordon Bonnet & Sarah Miller

CONTENTS

Thanks to Terry Curley for giving me permission to fictionalize his story about one odd and funny day at the firing range.

TO STOP A COCKFIGHT

THEY WERE A VERY FAMOUS couple. He was a world-renowned artist and a drunk, she was just as well known for her extravagant and highly destructive emotional breakdowns. They would roar into a town—New York, Los Angeles, Paris—like a whirlwind. Exuding charm and sophistication and displaying a world class penchant for alcohol, drugs, and histrionics, they would inevitably become embroiled in some sort of dust up with the locals that typically led to his arrest or detainment and a trip to rehab for her. It was all a lot of lovely fun, and they were frightfully good at it.

"Let's go to Havana," she proposed one evening when they had become fully bored with New York and had worn out their welcome there anyway. "We can get a room by the water and have wonderful parties every night. Champagne, fresh sea food, fresh people."

"Sounds swell, but I'm supposed to be finishing a painting this week. We'll need that big payday."

"Can't you just get an advance? You're good for it. You can finish it when we get back."

She sidled up next to him and slipped a hand down the front of his pants.

"Ooh," he moaned.

"Please," she whispered into his ear. He twisted under her sensual assault. "It'll be worth your while."

"No doubt," he said huskily.

"Now, call your stupid agent or the gallery and get us some money for Cuba." She slowly pulled her hand back out of his slacks. "I'm going to pack."

"Right this minute?"

"Unless you have something better in mind." She held her hand out toward him.

"You're taunting me."

"You're boring me."

"Let me come help you pack."

"Packing it is what you like best, right, baby?"

"Get up there, and you'll find out."

"You get up," she mocked.

With a wild roar, he chased her up the stairs to their spacious bedroom. She was still laughing when he caught her and wrestled her onto the bed.

"You are so easy," she said.

"You've been reading the tabloids again, haven't you?"

"TMZ." She giggled. "I saw it on TMZ."

———————————

THROUGH FRIENDS IN THE ART community who had contacts among the Washington high muckety-mucks, he had wrangled visas for the two of them on the pretense they were part of an international artist exchange. He was banking on the government not realizing the exchange was a bogus program until after the trip and they were back in the states. He was sure Cuba wouldn't care. It would look good for their Open Borders Program, and the greenbacks he was known to throw around so loosely would be icing on the international visitors cake.

They arrived at the International Terminal of José Martí Airport around 8 p.m. and, after clearing Customs with a minimum of hassle, grabbed a taxi to the Hotel Cienfuegos near Havana Bay. Havana was still plenty warm and humid like any tropical Caribbean city would be even though it was evening.

"Welcome to Havana." The friendly, English-speaking clerk checked their passports and returned them with a smile. "Mr. and Mrs. Sheridan."

"Where can we find a good bar with happening people?"

"Oh, Carlton." Mrs. Sheridan feigned embarrassment. "We needn't go out the moment we arrive in town."

"*Au contraire, mon* Zoe. That's exactly when we should go out."

"He's such a *bon vivant,*" Zoe explained to the clerk as if it were a medical condition that might need quarantining.

"You might try the Floridita. It was the favorite place of Mr. Hemingway."

"Ah, yes," Carlton said dramatically, "good old Ernest. He knew all the right places to drink. And I, Carlton F. Sheridan, good old American *artiste,* shall follow in Papa's glorious steps."

"Glorious Papa killed himself with a shotgun," Zoe reminded Carlton.

The clerk averted his eyes from the flamboyant couple.

"And more's the tragedy for it." Carlton waved his arm wildly. "All the more reason to share a libation in the gray-bearded one's ex-drinking hole."

"Before we even drop our things off in the room and freshen up a bit?"

"Hardly, my dear. We will retire to our temporary lodgings and prepare for the evening's entertainment. We're not animals, are we?"

"Thank you, young man." Zoe took the key to their room. Carlton trundled off toward the lobby elevator.

"*A sus ordenes.*" The clerk made a lengthy appraisal of Zoe's considerable physical charms. "At your service."

Zoe winked at the clerk and followed after Carlton who was already engaged in a conversation with the elevator attendant.

———

"I DON'T SEE ANYTHING SO special about this place," Zoe said, seated at the bar in the Floridita.

"Like you can't see the life-sized statue of Papa by the bar down there?" Carlton pointed to their left. "I'm surprised somebody didn't stuff him and set him on a stool with a daiquiri in his hand."

"Ah, yes." Zoe didn't bother to look at the statue of Hemingway. "The world-famous daiquiris in the world-famous Floridita. I feel like I just got off the cruise boat. Can we get any more touristy, you suppose? Where the hell is that bartender?"

The bartender was nearby and quite accommodating. He made daiquiri after daiquiri for them even when he should have stopped. Neither of them could really handle their liquor, and they squawked and made fun of an old trio that played local music while they and other wealthy gringo patrons got perfectly sloshed.

Around midnight, tired of daiquiris, the Sheridans stumbled out of the Floridita into the moist Havana night. They managed to hawk down a taxi and were able to convey to him their desire for continued partying. The driver took them to an upscale drinkery down by the harbor where they encountered a lovely young working woman who was amenable to their off-menu desires—for agreed upon compensation, of course. Back at the hotel, the threesome found the Sheridan's bed to be quite adequate for energetic physical activity.

Zoe dreamily caressed the young woman's inner thigh. "Her skin is so brown and silky soft."

"Marcela," Carlton said, between kisses with their new companion. "Her name is Marcela."

"Yes. Marcela."

Marcela writhed beneath Zoe's touch and Carlton's deep kisses. They occupied her then at both top and bottom. She moaned with pleasure. The sheets on the bed twisted beneath the voluptuaries into a labyrinth of wet, soft fabric. Finally, they lay still, satiated.

"What we need," Carlton proclaimed, after some quarter of an hour of rest and quiet, "is something more to drink."

The women, sleeping in each other's arms, did not hear him, so he rang up the desk and ordered a bottle of whiskey and a magnum of red wine. While his wife and their consort slept, Carlton drank shot after shot of whiskey and used the red wine as a chaser. All went well until about dawn.

"Oh." He belched, stomach rumbling and rolling violently. "I feel sick."

Clambering out of bed, he caught his feet in the sheets and fell face first on the floor. Grunting, he drug himself toward the bathroom on skinned up hands and knees. On the bed, the women rolled away from each other but neither woke. Carlton kept pulling himself along and barely made it to the bathroom before unleashing a torrent of yellowish-red liquid into the commode. He hurled and hurled. When there was no more liquid left, he began to wretch, dryly, loudly. It finally woke Zoe up. She slowly wound her way off the bed and into a wobbly upright position.

"Oh." She held her aching head.

Through bleary eyes she saw Carlton emerge from the bathroom. Thin lines of blood covered his lower lip and chin. He was slightly bent and holding his stomach. Zoe stumbled toward him.

"Baby, baby, you're bleeding. You're bleeding out your mouth."

"Threw up." Carlton smeared the blood on his face with the back of his hand. "Sick."

Zoe screamed and retched herself. She fell to one knee and cried.

"No, baby," Carlton said. "Not now. Don't lose it now."

But it was too late. Zoe was in the throes of a nervous attack. She was on the floor, back arched above the damp carpet, eyes rolled back in her head. She made a sound like a low-decibel scream coming from too deep inside her to be fully released into the air. Carlton reached out for her but was so weak from vomiting that he simply fell unconscious by her side.

———————————

AROUND TEN-THIRTY IN THE morning, with the sun shining brightly into the hotel room, Carlton awoke. His throat burned like fire itself, and his chest rattled with every deep breath. Crawling, stumbling out of bed, he went straight for the only cure he knew—more alcohol. He found it in a nearly empty bottle of Scotch lying on the bathroom floor. He downed it with one long swig.

"What the hell?" Through watery red eyes, he noted dried blood stains on the floor.

He wobbled back out to the bedroom looking for Zoe and the girl they had picked up. The girl was nowhere to be seen, but Zoe lay on the carpet beside the bed in a fetal position. He knelt beside her.

"Wake up, baby, get up."

She pulled herself into a tighter ball and moaned lowly. He looked around the room for more alcohol and something to smoke. Finding neither, he called down to the front desk for room service. They would find the items for the gentleman right away they said. They would have a bellboy bring them straight up. They were happy to accommodate the lovely North American couple.

While he waited on his whiskey and cigarettes, Carlton surveyed the damage in the room. Nothing broken but everything tossed around, sheets on the floor, food containers on a table and by a chair. He looked through his billfold and Zoe's purse to see if the girl had robbed them. If she had, she had not taken much. That was a good thing.

After a few minutes, he managed to muster the strength to lift Zoe and put her in bed. She stayed curled up like a baby, and he pulled the sheets over her to provide some decency for when room service arrived. There were the amenities to be accounted for after all.

She woke around noon, well after the whiskey and cigarettes arrived and had been paid for. Carlton still felt like hell, but the whiskey dulled the pain in his throat and chest, and he nursed Zoe most of the day. As soon as she was properly awake, she went into a highly agitated, nervous state. She alternately cried and cursed Carlton. With each outburst he drank more, ordering another bottle late in the afternoon, as well as another pack of smokes. There was considerable consternation between them, much leveling of charges, uncountable accusations.

But by evening, things had begun to smooth over. She was less agitated. His throat and chest hurt less. It was time to go out again. Around nine-thirty they prepared for the evening, dressing elegantly as always yet barely looking at one another. Outside, they found the same *taxista* who'd ferried them about the night before and told him to find a bar that Papa had not frequented.

The zinc bar in the Hotel Parador was a long, straight rectangle, worthy of Hemingway but not in existence during his time in Havana. Carlton and Zoe plopped down about mid-bar and ordered scotch on the rocks—they were beginning the evening slow. After several more rounds, they grew tired of the staid atmosphere of the Parador and had their waiting *taxista* score a fifth of Johnnie Walker Black and some "special" smoking material that they partook of while the cabbie drove aimlessly through the dark, moist Havana night. Despite the numbing effect of the alcohol and weed, Carlton's throat and chest continued to bother him, and between drinks and puffs he repeatedly hacked and coughed.

"You need a *medico?*" The cabbie turned around briefly.

"Wha...?" Zoe was slumped against the back seat away from Carlton.

"My throat hurts," Carlton said. "My chest."

"Cough medicine?" The cabbie suggested.

"Percodan, for pain. Or Oxycontin."

"Shew," the cabbie whistled, "you have to see a *medico* for that, *señor.* "

"A doctor?" Zoe perked up. "We need a doctor."

"You know one?" Carlton asked the cabbie.

"I know one. But it cost you money."

"Let's go. I'm tired of hurting."

"Yeah." Zoe re-involved herself in the evening. "Let's see a doctor."

The cabbie took them to an especially poor part of town and hooked the couple up with a *medico* friend of his. Carlton produced two large de-nomination American bills and the doctor produced a small envelope with five pills in it.

"Only five?" The doctor looked away. Carlton laid another big bill down and received another three pills.

"A real bargain," the cabbie said.

"*Ganga,*" the doctor confirmed.

"Screw you." Carlton took two of the pills and downed them with a big swig of alcohol. Zoe reached for the pills, but he only gave her one. "We can use the others later, baby."

Twenty minutes later all the pain was gone. No physical pain, no psychic pain. Carlton felt strong and magnanimous. Zoe giggled into the Havana night as if she and it shared some special Zen knowledge. They were both living in the moment, and the moment was fine.

"Where next, baby?"

"Any place but another damned old Papa bar."

"No more Papa bars."

"Nor mama bars, either." Carlton wise-cracked.

"You are so clever, my sweet."

"I don't understand," the cabbie said.

"We want to go somewhere exciting," Zoe told him. "Somewhere different. Somewhere where tourists would never go."

"You want to go maybe to a hole-in-the-wall *cantina?*"

"No, no. A place with danger, thrills. Not boring."

"Danger, not boring."

"You know of such a place?"

"I don't know, *señora.*"

"I've got it," Carlton declared.

"What, what, darling?"

"A cockfight. Let's go to a cockfight."

"Splendid."

"No." The cabbie waved his hand side to side. "No cockfight. Dangerous for foreigners."

"That's exactly why we want to go," Carlton said.

"Exactly," Zoe echoed.

"No, no," the cabbie reiterated. "Not good."

"Perfect," Carlton insisted. "Take us to one right now."

He handed the cabbie a respectable American bill.

"*Sí, señor.*" The cabbie admired the money.

"Oh, how wonderful." Zoe said, wild-eyed.

Carlton celebrated with a big slug of Johnnie Walker.

The cabbie drove the *Americanos* out to the edge of Havana where he knew of a semi-respectable cockfighting arena—*la Gallera Matanza*. He hoped the not quite so respectable neighborhood of the arena would dissuade them from their craziness. It did not.

"Is this it?" Zoe was not impressed by the wooden building housing the fights. Even at night she could see paint peeling from the walls and from around a couple of small windows on the side.

"This is it," the cabbie said. "Maybe you want to go back to a nice bar in town?"

"No way in hell." Carlton stumbled out of the cab. "We're going in there and see the birdies do battle."

Zoe giggled and struggled out of the cab.

"I better take you in," the cabbie said. "It can get a little rough."

Inside the *gallera*, most of the bettors—all men save a couple women standing in the shadows at the back of the arena—ignored the new arrivals except for a few whistles and catcalls aimed at Zoe as she and Carlton struggled to find a good viewing spot. The cabbie found a place behind them and tried to discreetly blend in. For his part, Carlton kept slamming down the Johnnie Walker and joined in the loud cheering of the crowd as two fighting birds were brought out for the next contest.

"Look how bright they are," Zoe commented. "They're beautiful."

"Very beautiful." Carlton swayed against the wood railing. He caught himself just before he would have fallen into the dirt of the arena floor. Two nearby men roughly pushed him back.

"Keep your hands off," he said drunkenly.

"Carlton," Zoe warned. "Don't start anything."

Before Carlton could come up with a response to Zoe, a roar from the crowd signaled the beginning of the fight.

One man in the ring acted as judge or referee while two other men held their fighting cocks up so that the birds could see each other. The animals immediately tried to peck each other. The audience cheered again. The judge then drew a line in the sandy floor of the arena, and the bird handlers placed their birds on it. The judge signaled with his right hand, and the men released the birds. It was as if chaos had been instantly unleashed in the building. Betting, cheering, jostling erupted on all sides, and the birds leaped and pecked at each other while trying to slice each other up with the sharp metal spurs attached to their feet.

At first Carlton and Zoe were into the fight. The birds were agile and courageous, fighting without taking or giving quarter. Feathers flew in all directions, with an occasional spray of chicken blood mixed in. Carlton looked down and saw some of the blood on his jacket and began howling insensibly. The combat thrilled Zoe and excited her until suddenly one of the cocks began to get the upper hand in the fight.

With a daring, athletic leap, one cock brought his spur against the neck of the other and slit a wound across its body, causing blood to fly all over the arena. As the wounded cock staggered backwards, the more powerful bird spun again and sliced the tendons on the back-left leg of his opponent. The injured bird reeled to one side, falling in the blood-spattered sand. It struggled back to one foot, but the other dangled in the air. The crowd roared. The sight of the cut and dying cock horrified Zoe.

"Stop it, stop it," she screamed at Carlton. "Stop them. It's horrible."

Dredging up energy from some long-forgotten place in his psyche and body, Carlton did as Zoe bid. He tried to leap over the railing, but his left leg didn't quite clear, and he landed chest-first into the sandy arena. Sliding in the sand and blood, Carlton struggled to his feet just as several men stormed into the ring after him. In seconds they were all over him—hitting, pummeling, kicking, biting, and gouging—trying to punish the insane foreign interloper who dared interfere with their game.

Carlton gamely but ineffectually tried to defend himself as the punches rained down on him from all directions. He was shoved and pushed back against the wood barrier of the arena. His assailants repeatedly hit him in the face and torso until he finally fell, Zoe shrieking madly as Carlton, unconscious, bounced off the floor of the arena. Several men drug him out and tossed his inert body on the dirty floor. More people kicked him while he was down. Zoe slapped at the men, but they spun her around in all directions, some of them pawing her breasts and pinching her buttocks.

Finally, the cabbie broke through the crowd and mercifully helped them toward the front door. Carlton regained consciousness as they reached it, and the cabbie helped him out just behind Zoe's fleeing form. The cabbie opened the back door of his vehicle, and Zoe threw herself inside. Carlton stumbled in behind her. Back at the *gallera,* it was all loud cheering and laughter.

"I told you we should not go there." The cabbie cranked the taxi engine and roared away from the cockfight arena.

"Shut up," Zoe cried, "you're a bastard just like all these people down here. Get us back to the hotel right now."

"*Sí, señora,* as you wish."

———————————

BACK AT THE HOTEL, CARLTON alternately threw up blood and passed out. His face was a mish-mash of cuts and bruises. After one particularly strong retching episode, he collapsed on the floor of the bathroom, and Zoe thought he might have died. In a panic she called the main desk and blubberingly demanded a doctor be sent up immediately. Carlton's breathing was shallow and slow when the doctor arrived. Zoe helped lift Carlton onto the bed where the doctor examined him.

"He's going to die," Zoe said. The doctor couldn't tell if it was a question or a statement.

"He is in a bad way," he told her. "Perhaps he will not die."

"What are you going to give him?" She watched the doctor remove a small, dark bottle from a well-used, brown leather bag. He stuck a syringe into the end of the bottle and drew out a slightly yellow but otherwise clear liquid.

"This is Vitamin B6." The doctor squirted some liquid from the syringe to eliminate any air bubbles. "It should make your *esposo* much better."

Within a quarter hour of the injection, Carlton began to stir back to life. Zoe overpaid the doctor with the promise he would return at once if needed. After getting another type of liquid into Carlton, this time plain old boring water, Zoe settled him comfortably in bed. She nervously paced the room until sure he was breathing safely. Right away he drifted back off, and when she was sure he was just sleeping and not dead, she curled up under a blanket in one of the room's chairs and fell into a troubled sleep.

Late in the afternoon of the following day, with Carlton out of immediate danger but still barely mobile, Zoe had the hotel main desk order first class air tickets for New York and call a taxi to drive them to the airport.

In New York, he was hospitalized for alcohol poisoning and exhaustion. Zoe left him on the third day of his treatment and flew home to be with her mother in Georgia. In a matter of days word came that Carlton had died of liver failure. It surprised Zoe that the news failed to move her. All she could remember was him lying on the hotel floor barely breathing.

In time, even the indifference faded. She moved on with her life. Without Carlton she found, surprisingly, that she could paint. Her bold slashes of brazen, bright colors brought critical praise. She worked steadily, even feverishly—allowed herself to be absorbed by her art.

At times, she remembered the earlier, better days with Carlton. Rarely, she felt a twinge of guilt for having left him alone in New York. He was in such bad shape and she had never seen him alive again. Despite everything, she had once cared and would have liked to have said goodbye.

They had loved one another, each in their own way, but her only hope for personal survival was to escape. To get away. To avoid the entropic spiral that was Carlton F. Sheridan. There was an occasional dark place where he used to be, but she learned to move past it. She had to. For her own sanity, her life, her art.

THREE DAYS

THE DAY BEFORE HE AND a couple of his buddies from Wing HQ were to leave for Tokyo on a special three-day R&R, Frank Mason's lower left wisdom tooth started acting up. Next morning it was sore as hell, and his jaw was swollen up like he was chewing a small cud of tobacco.

"Damn," he complained to Coleman and Upshaw as they crossed the flight line to board a C-130 transport for Tachikawa, "my tooth's killing me."

"Maybe you should go later," Coleman suggested.

"Sarge'll let you go on another one," Upshaw said.

"I ain't takin' the chance. If I don't go now, I might not ever get to. They might change it on me."

"I don't know, man," Coleman said, "you may not have much fun."

"It'll ease up."

"It's all swole up," Upshaw said for Coleman's benefit, "like a summer tick on a fat hound dog."

"Nothin's keepin' me from this R&R," Mason insisted over his buddies' laughter and the roar of C-130 engines. "I'm having fun no matter what. I got the money, I got the time, we got our orders. I got some pain pills from the medics. I'm going if it kills me."

"You been lucky lately anyway," Upshaw said. "Maybe it'll get better."

"I can't believe you pulled that $150 pot the other night," Coleman said as they reached the plane.

An E-4 gave their orders a quick look before letting them on board.

"Me, neither."

Mason thought back to the big Acey-Deucey card game two nights before. He vividly recalled the sweaty, feverish moment when he put $150 on the table—just shy of two full weeks of pay at E-4, over three years in service, overseas and per diem combined—matching the pot. Three hundred dollars. And the double deck had run out. Larrabee was dealing, and he had the touch for burning people. Mason had an ace and a deuce. The best you could have.

Larrabee shuffled, Woods cut, everybody held their breath. Mason felt like his heart had stopped. Larrabee tossed down a seven. Not even close. Everybody got really excited. Mason thought he was going to faint. He pulled in the three hundred dollars. Incredible. Then Larrabee showed the cards on either side of Woods's cut. A deuce and an ace. One card in either direction and Mason would've been stone broke.

Instead he was rich. And on his way to Japan, back to where he'd spent two years already. Although this time down south, at Tachi. No frozen north, but Tokyo, the imperial palace, the Ginza. A practically infinite number of bars and women.

"Hot damn," he said through closed teeth. "We gonna have us some fun."

He fingered a wad of bills in his pocket and again relished his victory. But the wad was considerably smaller than it had been two nights ago. He'd already lost $65 of his winnings on slot machines in the Airman's Club in Korea. Still it was a substantial roll. He clambered into the interior of the C-130 with Upshaw and Coleman. He let them think he still had all his winnings. He was sure his luck hadn't really run out yet.

———————

SINCE THE C-130 WASN'T RIGGED for people, Mason and his buddies sat on the big back door of the plane among a collection of jeeps, tires, and what looked like parts for tanks. There were a couple of rows of harness seats on either side of the plane, but except for one burly Staff Sergeant courier and a Japanese officer, they were also filled with supplies.

In the center of the craft were maybe eight or ten long narrow metal boxes. With American casualties in the war running at their highest levels ever, it didn't take a genius to figure out what was in or going to be in the boxes.

Unconsciously clamping, releasing, clamping, and re-releasing his aching jaw muscles, Mason pretended he couldn't see the boxes. Through the haze of his pain, he tried to concentrate on Coleman telling the E-4 why they were in Korea.

"...after they captured the *Pueblo,* they shipped our whole base over here. It went from about twelve hundred guys to nearly six thousand in three days." The E-4 whistled appreciatively. "We been living in tents and working twelve hours a day since we got here. Hell, we was all restricted to base for the first six weeks. It looked like another war was coming. Man, we're sandbagged in to the hilt."

"How come you guys are going with us back to Japan?"

"R&R. We all work at Wing HQ." He pointed to Upshaw and Mason. "One of our sergeants wangled it for us. Hell, we can go anywhere. These orders we got don't have a destination on them."

"No kidding. I didn't even pay any attention."

"Yeah, we're up there with all the brass. We got this Colonel Y...."

Mason tuned the conversation out. He was feeling poorly, and Coleman's BS wasn't going to help. Upshaw noticed Mason looked wobbly.

"Hey, dude, you all right?"

"Huh?" Mason answered from his fog.

"You okay?"

"Yeah. . . just hurts, that's all."

"Whyn't you take some of them pills Doc give you? Maybe they'd help."

"Not yet. I don't need 'em."

"Couldn't hurt."

"I'll wait."

Mason held both hands against the sides of his face, putting pressure on the jaws. When he released the pressure, his bad jaw didn't hurt so much. He did that off and on for ten or fifteen minutes, all the time staring at the floor. Coleman and the E-4 kept talking. Upshaw read the Stars and Stripes newspaper.

After a while, Mason got up and walked over to a small window by one of the big side doors and peered out. They must be getting close to Japan, he figured, watching a collection of tiny green islands go by. He watched the islands for several minutes until a sharp pain pushed him to walk some more.

He went up toward the cockpit, then back along the side where he'd looked out the window, looped past his buddies, and sidled through the metal coffins up to where the Staff Sergeant and the Japanese officer sat several yards apart.

With a closer look, Mason could tell from the officer's uniform that he was from the Japanese Air Self-Defense Force. Two years of seeing the off-blue khakis and the geometric-like rank on the shoulder plates made the ID easy. Mason tried a smile at the officer. The officer looked back impassively. He carried a U.S. handgun, not a .45 but a standard barrel .38, in a holster hooked to the back of his uniform like the many U.S. pilots Mason had seen strutting along the flight line in Korea.

Mason looked around and rubbed his jaw. He considered starting a conversation, but the JASDF officer seemed to be frowning at him. Mason felt the bottle of pain pills in his fatigue shirt. The JASDF officer turned quickly toward him. Surprised, Mason jumped back.

The officer reached beneath a blue coat he carried on his lap. For a split-second Mason thought he saw the flash of another blue barrel. It happened so quickly, and the JASDF officer was motionless again so rapidly, Mason immediately doubted what he'd seen. Why would the damned JASDF pull a gun on him, anyway? It was crazy.

He must've just thought he'd seen it. A hallucination. That idea really made him feel out of balance. With a peek back at the JASDF, he walked slowly, uncertainly away. He took two of the pain pills out of his pocket and swallowed them without water. He nearly gagged. He wished like hell that they would get to Tachi. He felt like drinking a quart of Johnnie Walker all by himself.

After a couple of minutes, in which he took several, what he hoped were surreptitious, glances back at the officer, he realized his escape from the JASDF had put him right up next to the Staff Sergeant courier. This guy was truly massive, from the top of his too-small hat to the tips of his patent leather-shiny black brogans. He was carrying a .45. It was holstered thickly and awesomely at his more than ample side.

The briefcase the courier watched over was hooked to him by about a foot of link chain attached to one big wrist by a handcuff. The courier had a broad, flat forehead, bushy eyebrows, a crooked—no doubt many times broken—nose, and a jaw doing a good impression of human rock. Through blurring eyes, he saw that the courier was reading something.

He moved a little closer and squinted to see what it was. It was a Popeye comic. Off and on the courier would laugh heartily, slowly turning the pages. The courier looked up and grinned. He was missing a couple of front teeth.

Mason suppressed a laugh and almost farted. This guy must be the perfect courier, he thought. No one in their right mind would get anywhere near that briefcase as long as that guy was hooked to the other end of it.

Smiling feebly, he backed away from the courier, walking back over to the side of the plane to look out. Even though the pills were already affecting him, his jaw still hurt, his ears were plugging up—he hadn't noticed they'd begun their descent—and he was picking up a case of what looked like it might be bad gas. He felt like crap. He was entertaining the idea that he'd already died and gone to hell.

As proof of his new theory, the C-130 suddenly hit a pocket of bad air and dropped a couple of hundred feet. He felt like he was going to lose what was left of his breakfast. The smell of half-digested eggs filled his nostrils. He belched loudly.

With an effort, he managed to make it back to his seat on a tire between Upshaw and Coleman. Upshaw gave him a concerned once over. Mason massaged his jaw and rocked back and forth on the tire. He figured that if this wasn't hell, it was damn close. Close enough for government work, anyway.

———————

BY THE TIME THEY SETTLED into the Bachelor Airmen's Quarters at Tachikawa, Mason was in a darkening tunnel of drugs and pain. The spacious Quonset hut BAQ held none of the charm it had just over a year ago when he'd passed through on his rotation back to the world.

While Coleman and Upshaw cleaned up for a big night out, he took two more pills and lay on his cot staring at some bugs that may or may not have been crawling around on the ceiling. As he drifted off, he saw himself standing astride two rows of metal boxes on a flight line somewhere in some distant jungle. The boxes were moving around under his feet, and he was fighting to keep them still.

"Mason." Upshaw woke him a quarter of an hour later. "Mason. Get up. We be goin' down to the USO center in Tokyo. Come on, get up."

"Wha..?" Mason stirred, drug himself back into consciousness. Upshaw helped him sit up.

"How you feelin', dude? I thought you was dead."

"Oh, oh... uh, better. Where we going?"

"The USO center down by the Ginza, some dudes here told us about it. It's real cheap, and we can leave our bread with them so we don't be gettin' broke the first night."

"Is he going?" Coleman came in from the hallway into their sleeping area of the modular quonset hut.

Each of Tachi's BAQ huts were divided into six or seven sections with cots for six men in each section.

"I'm going." Mason stood up slowly. "Nothing stops me from having fun. These pills are doing all right. I'll be okay."

"Great," Coleman said, "let's blow this joint and act like civvies for a couple of days. Wooo-ee. Tokyo! The Ginza! Booze and poontang till hell freezes over."

"Hot damn," Upshaw cheered, "we be partyin' now, oh, hot damn."

———————

MASON SAT AT THE BAR of the Flaming Tiger night club, trying to remember if he'd left his money in the safe back at the USO hotel or if he'd already spent all but $70 of the over $200 he'd brought. He grimaced and tried to focus on the inside of his billfold. He knew he'd broken a twenty for some drinks—rum and coke—a couple for him, a couple for a cute girl who hung around him until she saw him drop two more of the pain pills.

"You messed up, GI."

She drifted away from him when he spilled his drink reaching for her.

The last two pills, augmented by the rum, started to kick in. He ordered a fresh rum and coke and paid for it with a ten he found in his pocket. The bartender wiped up the mess on the counter, brought the new drink and the change in yen and set them in front of him.

"*Arigato,*" Mason slurred.

He felt really hot. The red flame decor of the bar didn't help much, either. He wiped his forehead with the cool drops from the side of the drink.

"Look, dude." Coleman came up to the bar with a pretty Japanese girl. "Look over there, dude, round-eyed poon." He pointed to a table in a corner across the room. There were three Caucasian women at the table. "Check it out, man."

"Yeah."

"Well, go get it. Go on."

"Go on."

"Move it." Coleman pushed Mason away from the bar. "Don't be a jerk." He stumbled and swiped at his drink, somehow snagging it as he awkwardly and somewhat reluctantly made his way toward the table of women. Coleman and the girl watched from the bar.

"How you doin'?" He asked the women when he finally reached them.

He stood there, wavering, leaning slightly to one side. The women chatted on among themselves. In his fog, he was able to make out that all three were good looking with unusually short hair.

He thought they must be service girls. He cleared his throat. Two of the girls talked on, ignoring him. The other, a curly haired brunette, looked up at him.

"Uh," he repeated, "how you doin'?"

"Hello," the brunette said amiably.

The girl next to her, a sandy blonde, gave Mason a quick glance, then went back to talking with the other girl.

"H—H—Hi," Mason stuttered.

The brunette watched him with more than a little amusement.

"Are you a GI?"

He looked at her as if he'd just seen her for the first time. He struggled to clear his head.

"Yeah." He lit a cigarette and offered one to the girl, which she turned down. "Over here from Korea."

"Oh, R&R. This your first time overseas?"

"Naw." Mason sipped his drink while smoke boiled from his nostrils. "Was here before. Up north. Near Aomori."

"We've been up there." The girl pointed to her friends. "It's nice."

"You all in the service?"

The woman talking to the blonde, a stocky, midwestern-looking brunette laughed. Mason focused on her.

"No," the first brunette said, "we're USO."

"Oh."

He looked at the blonde, then at the stocky brunette again. Hard as it was for him to evaluate anything at the moment, he felt they were making fun of him.

"Can I buy you a drink?"

"Thanks, but no," the first brunette said, "we're fine for now." The other two women giggled.

"C'mon, I'll buy you a beer." He waved for a barmaid. All three of the women were watching him now. "You guys need a drink."

"Us guys don't need anything from you, guy," the stocky girl said. Mason looked at her and suppressed a belch.

"Thanks, anyway," the friendly girl told him.

"I'll get you one," he said, as the barmaid came up. "Three beers."

The barmaid left. He faced the three women.

"Thanks for the beers," the nice one said, "but we're just together, the three of us."

"Great."

The barmaid brought the beers. Mason managed to find a twenty and gave it to the woman. A "hostess" watching him and the women moved into range. No one said anything for a while. He just stood there in his reddish haze.

"It was nice talking to you," the nice woman said. "Bye."

"Uh—I...."

"Goodbye," the blonde said sharply. Mason's head jerked back at the tone of her voice.

"Huh?"

"Scram," the blonde said, "see you around."

"Hey, you know what...."

"Split," the stocky girl told him.

He wasn't sure what he'd done wrong. He didn't know why these women were mad at him.

"Get lost, buster," the stocky one said, "Beat it."

She turned away and began talking to the blonde again. He looked at the nice brunette. She acted like she was watching something on the other side of the room.

"Well, hell. I'll be a sonofabitch."

He left with the women's laughter in his ears. The "hostess" tried to take his arm. He pushed her away and found Coleman at the bar with the girl.

"Well," Coleman said, "how did it go?"

"They ain't lookin' for guys."

"Huh, I don't get it."

"What can I say." Mason popped another set of pain pills and ordered a fresh beer. He realized that his jaw wasn't hurting a bit. "My tooth feels great."

"I don't know what you mean," Coleman said.

"I mean it don't hurt."

"No, no, about the women."

"What do you think it means?"

"Oh."

"I feel like hell."

"You're just messed up now."

"Where's Lonnie?"

"He already split with a chick."

"Jerk."

"Why don't you go with us?" Coleman indicated his girl. "We're gonna hit a coupla more bars before we go to her place. What'ya say?"

"Why not?" Mason opened his eyes wide to keep them from closing. "Why the hell not?"

———————

WHEN MASON'S HEAD CLEARED, HE was in another bar sitting at a table with a relatively young, nice-looking girl.

"Where the hell is this?"

"The Naraka bar," she told him. "You lots drunk, ney?"

He looked around the bar. There were only another couple or two, Japanese and a scrawny little old man tending bar.

"Where's Coleman? I was with him and his girl."

"You mean you friend?"

"Yeah, where is he?"

"They go already, do some bang bang."

"Oh."

He felt in his shirt pocket for the pain pills. They were gone. He checked his pants. Gone.

"Hell."

"Go now?"

"What?"

"We go my place now. Go do it."

"Yeah, okay. Let's go."

Outside, the girl hawked down a burnt orange cab. She said something to the driver, and he reached over and opened the back door from the inside. The girl stood by the door watching Mason. He was breathing in the night air, trying to get straight.

"Pay now." The girl pointed to the driver.

"Now?"

"Now."

He dug around in his pockets but only came up with a couple of military payment certificate one dollar bills.

"You billfold."

Mason pulled it out. He had an MPC ten and a greenback five. He couldn't believe it was all he had left.

"How much?" He asked the driver, keeping the wallet away from the girl's sight.

"Ten."

He wondered if the cabby had seen in his billfold. He started to get the money out, but the girl grabbed the wallet away from him.

"Hey, give it back."

"This all you got?"

"Give it here."

"You number ten GI."

Mason was afraid she'd get the local cops on him. He remembered near-

ly getting robbed by a woman and her neighbors in a back alley in Korea.
All he wanted now was out of this place.

He'd lost all his money, his head hurt, and he felt nauseated. He reached
for the billfold. The girl grabbed the greenback five and threw the billfold in
his face. It bounced off him and landed on the curb.

"Filthy, cheap GI."

"Jesus, it's all I got left."

He stooped to pick up the contents of his wallet. The girl spat at him,
missed, and ran off down the street exclaiming loudly in Japanese. He re-
trieved the billfold and stood up, then leaned against the cab and sighed.

"You still want taxi?"

Mason took a deep breath and slowly released it. For the second time
that day it occurred to him he might have already died and gone to hell.

"Okay, you know the USO center near the Ginza."

"I know."

"Great."

Mason got in the cab and collapsed onto the back seat.

"Ten dollar." The driver reached his hand over the seat.

Mason pulled out his wallet. He handed over the MPC ten.

"No, dollar?"

"All I got. MPC."

"MPC not so good."

"Give it back, then. I'll walk."

The cabby thought it over for a moment.

"I take MPC." He steered the taxi out into the thinning late-night traffic.

"Hell, yes."

As the vehicle sped through the neon exuberance of Tokyo, Mason
leaned his head back on the seat and closed his eyes. He felt like he was
drifting again. He didn't know where he was, his jaw was starting to ache
again, and he'd lost his pain pills. Things weren't looking so good. He was
already broke, and there were still two days of R&R to go.

AT THE FIRING RANGE

BYRNES AND MILLER KNEW THEIR unit had to qualify on the firing range the next morning, but they went downtown on a drinking spree, anyway.

They downed beers for a couple of hours in one bar, shots of straight whiskey in a second, and cups of hot sake in a third. By curfew they were beyond three sheets to the wind. As they stumbled back toward the main gate, Miller realized he was hungry.

"I'm starving. I gotta eat."

"We'll get something back at the snack bar." Byrnes weaved dangerously close to the edge of the sidewalk curb.

"No, here's a place. Let's stop. I'm hungry."

"All right." Byrnes was hungry, too.

They stopped in front of the restaurant, a Japanese place that served seafood, noodle soup, and their favorite meal, a big, juicy, open-faced hamburger with a fried egg on top. While waiting for the burger, Miller opted for a batch of miniature shrimp as an appetizer, a delicacy Byrnes declined. By the time they had polished off the eggburger, they were beginning to sober up. Miller let loose a loud belch, complaining about the strong smell of his egg.

Lumbering out into the night air again, they grabbed some beers at a little joint near the main gate and guzzled those. That corrected the sobering up part. By the time they got back to the barracks, neither of them remembered anything about having to qualify the next morning. They were completely hammered.

———————————

EDMONDS THE JEEP, A RECENT arrival on base in the jargon of the unit, came bustling into the barracks about six thirty a.m. He was excited.

"Hey." He shook Byrnes's shoulders to get him awake. "Today's qualifying day. We gotta be at the range by seven fifteen. Sergeant Lawson's already outside, and he's raising hell gettin' everybody up. Come on, dude, hustle. He'll kill us. Come on."

"Geez." Byrnes squinted against the light of the new day.

"You gotta get up."

"Leave me alone."

Edmonds tried to wake Byrnes again, who swung feebly at the younger man. Edmonds easily avoided the punch and laughing, helped Byrnes sit up.

"Oh, man, my head hurts like hell."

"Want an aspirin?"

"About ten of them, and the hair of the dog that bit me."

Byrnes looked over at a stand beside his cot. There actually was a bottle of whiskey there, with a few drops in it.

"Get me those aspirins."

Edmonds hustled out, returning in just a few moments with the aspirin. Byrnes was sitting up on the edge of the bed now.

"Thanks, man. Thanks." He took two of the offered aspirins and swallowed the rest of the whiskey. "Oh, geez." He groaned, the alcohol coursing roughly down his throat and into his booze-logged system. For just a moment, he felt like he might throw up. Then it passed. "You say old Lawson is down there?"

"Yeah, and he's heading this way after he rousts the guys in the other barracks. You better get going."

"I'll be fine." Byrnes slowly stood up. "After I take a quick shower. Get Miller up."

"You guys hit the town last night?"

"Does a bear shit in the woods? Get going. Lawson ain't too keen on Miller lately anyway. Make sure he's up and gets a fast shower. He'll be all right."

"Okay." Edmonds hustled away.

"Ow." Byrnes rolled his head around and rubbed the back of his neck. "Damned qualifying day."

Miller was in worse shape than Byrnes when Edmonds found him moments later.

"Leave me the hell alone," Miller growled at the bright-eyed youngster.

"Sergeant Lawson is coming, and Byrnes said I should get you up right away. Have you take a shower."

"Byrnes can go to hell, too." Miller rolled away and pulled covers over his head. Edmonds would not be denied. He would rather face Miller's wrath than Sergeant Lawson's.

Any time.

"You have to get up, dude. We have to qualify today. We have to be at the firing range by seven fifteen."

"My head is killing me. My tongue hurts, and my teeth are asleep."

"What?"

"Shelley Berman." Miller coughed and lifted himself up in the bed.

"Who's he?"

"Never mind. You must be too young."

"You must be hungover, too."

"You must be Sherlock Holmes. You know who he is, don't you?"

"Sure, I know him."

"Great, just great."

"Byrnes took some aspirin and the skin of the dog that bit him." Edmonds mangled the old saying.

"What?" Miller tried to laugh. He stopped. The effort hurt too much. "Hair of the dog, Edmonds. Hair of the dog."

"Oh." Edmonds held out a hand with aspirins in it. "I have some more here. I can get you a beer or something."

"God, no. I'll just get up and shower and get ready."

"Okay. I'll meet you guys out front. The bus'll be there."

"Great." Miller groaned.

"What's the matter?"

"My guts are killing me."

"Can I help?"

"Out of the way." Miller suddenly leapt from his cot.

Edmonds barely got out of the way as Miller rushed down the barracks hallway and sped into the latrine howling.

"Whoa." Edmonds said out loud to the empty hallway. "Man, oh, man."

After five minutes of moaning and groaning, Miller stumbled back out into the barracks proper. Sergeant Lawson was waiting on him.

"You about ready to join the rest of the ladies, Miller?" the old warhorse of an NCO said wryly.

"My stomach ain't doing too well, Sarge."

"No lie, smells like something crawled up inside you and died, boy."

"I don't think I'm up to the qualifying, Sarge."

"You're goin', Miller, if I have to cart a latrine out to the range for you. This was supposed to be a day off for me, and by God, if I have to go, then every single one of you is going, too. That's final."

"Yes, Sergeant, I'll get on my fatigues."

"That would be the uniform of the day. Now get a move on."

Everyone, including Sergeant Lawson, was on the bus waiting for Miller when he finally made his way onto the vehicle. He sat down next to Byrnes, who was wearing non-regulation sunglasses to block the sunlight from his aching eyes.

"I feel like hell." Miller said. Byrnes grunted.

The bus lurched forward, and the driver, a nervous E-4 from motor pool, made more uneasy with gruff Sergeant Lawson sitting imperiously at his back, headed the big blue bus down the street in front of the barracks and on past some nearby buildings.

"Did you eat anything yet?" Miller looked out as the bus lugged past the group's chow hall.

"God, no," Byrnes said, "I'd probably puke it up."

Miller groaned, his stomach rolling at the thought of the regurgitation process.

He belched loudly, fighting back an impulse to throw up. The bitter, acrid taste of last night's alcohol and late meal replayed itself in his mouth and nearly caused a rather unpleasant reflex action. The belch was followed by flatulation loudly broadcast over the immediate area.

"Jesus Christ." Byrnes held his nose with a thumb and forefinger. "What was that? My, God."

"Sorry, man, I can't help it. It must've been something we ate last night."

"I don't even remember what we ate last night." Byrnes slid in the seat to avoid the foul remains of Miller's fart.

At the first intersection past the chow hall, a four way stop, the bus died.

"What the hell's the matter now," Sergeant Lawson bellowed at the shaky E-4.

"N—nothing, Sarge, it… it just died."

"Get it started."

"Yes, sir."

"And don't call me sir. I work for a living, sonny."

"Yes, s—uh, yes."

After several grinding attempts, the bus coughed and boomed and chugged back into motion. The driver smiled weakly at Sergeant Lawson. The sergeant did not reciprocate.

A gusting wind and more delays greeted them at the firing range. The sergeant in charge was nowhere to be seen. The rifles and ammunition were locked up safely in a large shed, and there was nothing to do but wait. The wind whipped and swirled, throwing bits of grass and dirt around.

During the wait, Miller's stomach got worse. It seemed to be doing flip flops inside his body.

"I feel really bad," he told Byrnes about ten minutes into the wait. "Do you see a latrine around here, man?"

"I don't think there is one." Byrnes rubbed his temples and eyes behind the dark shades.

"Damn it. I need to take a crap."

"Tell Lawson. I can't do anything about it."

"Yeah, right."

After about another ten minutes, the sergeant in charge of the range finally showed up, holding onto his hat in the wind.

"My apologies, Eldon," he told Lawson. "Late night at the NCO Club. You understand."

"Just get this damned range open, Barrett. You are wasting my time here."

"Geez, no need to take it out on me. I got here as soon as I could."

"Get on with it."

Sergeant Barrett hustled around the range then, opened the shed, got the men to take fresh paper targets out in the field for the firing. He had others bring out the weapons and ammo and did an efficient, brisk job of getting the place ready for Lawson's minions.

Out at the targets, there were more problems. The wind was blowing just hard enough to make placing the paper targets onto their stands a real problem. No sooner would a guy get his target up than it would tear on one side, start flapping, and next thing he knew it would be blowing across the range or slapping back and forth against the stand.

"Damn it." Byrnes jabbed some small sticks he found on the ground into his target and then watched the paper rip away and flap wildly in the wind. "Crap."

"Here." Edmonds brought Byrnes a stapler he'd found somewhere. "Use this."

"Now you're talking." Byrnes secured his target with four well-placed staples. "You did good, Jeep."

"Uh, yeah, thanks. I think."

"This stuff is soft when you touch it." Miller fondled one of the targets.
Byrnes and Edmonds looked at each other with raised eyebrows.

"Oh, yeah," Byrnes said, "smooth as silk."

"It beats corn cobs or leaves," Miller countered.

"Yeah." Byrnes drug the word out to about three syllables.

"I'm just saying." Miller said.

"We got 'em all now." Edmonds looked up and down the line of targets.
"We better get back up to Sarge."

Finally, everything seemed to be in place. The two sergeants got the
men squared away up and down the line. Everyone had an M-16 and three
clips of ammo. It was time to qualify, wind and delays be damned.

"Gentlemen," Sergeant Lawson told his troops, the irony in the expres-
sion of that word so thick that even the densest among them understood it,
"obey my every command. Fire only on my order. Stop immediately when I
say stop. This can be painless for all of us, if even a little loud."

Edmonds raised his hand.

"What is it?"

"Sarge, what about ear protection. My ears are sensitive."

"Sergeant Barrett," Sergeant Lawson seethed, "will provide ear plugs for
anyone whose puny-ass ears can't take the sound."

"Thank you, Sergeant."

"We will fire first from the prone position." Sergeant Lawson had Sergeant Barrett distribute ear plugs to Edmonds and a handful of other men.

"We should've got us some of those," Miller said under his breath to
Byrnes, who was next to him on the firing line.

"Shut up, he'll kill the next guy who says anything or messes up."

"My guts are killing me."

"Get into the prone position," Sergeant Lawson called out.

All the men, save Miller, were quickly on their stomachs. For Miller, the
act of trying to get prone was asking too much. His stomach was absolutely
churning. He knew he couldn't last much longer.

"Is the line ready on the left?" Sergeant Lawson faced the firing range.

"Ready on the left," Sergeant Barrett declared as if he were in charge of that side of the firing line. Sergeant Lawson glared at him and started to say something but held back.

"Is the line ready on the ri—"

Suddenly, Miller waved his arms back and forth.

"Hold it," he cried, "hold it."

"What the hell?" Sergeant Lawson said.

The men looked up from their positions. A couple of them tittered, some turned away, others looked out at the targets on the range where a few were beginning to flap dangerously, threatening to become airborne.

"Oh, God, Miller." Byrnes said. "Oh, man, what are you doing?"

Without regard to the lines of men lying there with weapons ready to fire and without hearing Sergeant Lawson scream for the unit to stand down, to lower their weapons, to hold their fire, and for Miller to stop where he was, Miller, with no apparent concern for his own personal safety or anything else, raced across the firing range, heading for the targets. He flailed his arms as he tore out onto the range. His fatigue hat, caught in a gust of wind, flew off into the dirt and grass of the range. He didn't stop to go back for it.

"Damn you, Miller." Sergeant Lawson shook his fist at the fleeing figure.

"What's he doing now?" A kid next to Byrnes said.

"He's got the shits." Byrnes grinned. "He's takin' a latrine break."

And sure enough, when Miller reached the targets he paused briefly, ripping one of the paper bulls-eyes off with his hands.

"Oh, man." Byrnes said. "Unbelievable."

Paper target in hand, Miller jogged past the target stands and leaped into a deep ditch behind them. A puff of dirt was momentarily visible but then drifted away on the wind. The ditch into which Miller disappeared ran in front of a built-up dirt hill that was several yards further back and which served as an earthen safety net for the many errant shots taken from the firing range. There was probably enough metal in that hill to build part of a B-52—or maybe *all* of one.

Back on the line, everyone was still, watching the spot beyond which Miller had disappeared. Nobody said anything. Not even Sergeant Lawson. A couple of guys yawned. Sergeant Barrett looked up at the sky and whistled. The sound was lost in the blowing wind. Byrnes looked down the line to his left and saw Edmonds. Edmonds waved at him. Byrnes looked back out across the range.

About seven or eight minutes after he made his desperate run, Miller suddenly popped back up on the backside of the targets. He held his hands up as if someone might still be thinking of firing in his direction. After another moment he began walking back toward the firing line. He walked slowly but calmly. He didn't seem to be desperate anymore. He even managed to catch his fatigue cap and put it back on properly. When he was nearly back to the firing line, he changed direction and walked toward Sergeant Lawson, who waited patiently for him.

"Uh, sorry, Sarge." He stood in a relaxed parade rest posture.

Sergeant Lawson didn't say a word. Miller walked back over to his position by Byrnes.

"Shall we continue?" Sergeant Barrett said after another pause.

"Sarge?" Miller said in another minute.

Sergeant Lawson appeared to be considering his next course of action. The men didn't know what the old warhorse would do. He might make them run laps around the range. He might actually punch Miller out. They had been made aware that this was to have been a day off for him and that he didn't appreciate their qualification getting in the way of a chance to escape the rigors of the base for a full weekend.

The old veteran of the brown shoe days and the Army-Air Corps scratched his chin and the side of his face and prepared to address his troops. They waited silently, ready to accept their fate. Only the wind made any sound. He cleared his throat.

"To hell with it, men." A tired resignation and grudging acceptance of defeat and ultimate surrender underlay his words. "Let's just pack it in."

There was a general shuffling and stumbling around as the men hustled to store their weapons and ammo before reboarding the bus. A couple of guys couldn't restrain giggles, but one look from Sergeant Lawson nipped those in the bud. In moments, they were back on the bus, glad to be out of the wind and filtering down the aisle without looking at each other. The motor pool driver started the big vehicle, and with a loud backfire and in a cloud of smoke it clanged on back toward the barracks.

The unit never did qualify that year and no one ever said anything about it. Nobody at the group or command level mentioned any such breach of military order. Sergeant Lawson, the pro's pro, acted as if nothing had ever happened. No one ever brought up the subject again. They didn't dare.

NAPALM NIGHT

"GIMME A HIT OF THAT, man," Zapper said, a light breeze finally bringing some respite from the day's heat and humidity.

Ofay handed the joint across after taking another huge drag.

"Aw, man, you got the end all wet, brother."

Ofay had gotten his nickname back in his first platoon, which except for him, was all white. Another brother had seen him and his group back in the rear on stand down and given him the ironic label. The name stuck and now Marvin T. Johnson was Ofay, to himself and to everybody else.

"Up yours, white boy."

Zapper chuckled and inhaled deeply from the thick, potent reefer. He took another couple of shallow puffs and passed the joint on.

There were five in the group, sitting off from the rest of the platoon. They were short-timers, dopers, when they had anything even vaguely resembling a stand down at the firebase. They were considered screw-ups, but they'd all been in-country at least nine months, and they were all still alive. No one argued against success.

Besides Zapper and Ofay, there was Bertoni, the platoon's radio operator, Muddy Freddy, an Arkansas hillbilly, and "Professor" Calvin, so named because he'd actually spent most of one academic year at the University of Minnesota.

"My turn, Mud," the professor prompted Freddy, who tended to Bogart joints to the extreme, "cough it up." Freddy grunted but surrendered the joint. Ofay started another one around.

"What a beautiful country this is, huh, dudes?" The professor swung an arm out before him, its sweep intended to encompass the shadowy valley that lay before them, with its occasional village, fields of rice, and winding muddy river.

"Practically a tourists' delight," Zapper said sardonically.

Ofay lit a third joint. The weed went round and round.

"I'm really zoned." Bertoni wheezed after a couple of successive hits. "Anybody got anything to drink?"

Zapper pulled a beer out of a rucksack at his feet and pitched it to Bertoni. "Share it, man."

Bertoni popped the top, took a swig and handed the beer to Freddy.

"Ugh, warm Black Label. Lousy crap."

"Try to think of it as the grunt's Michelob, Mud," the professor said.

"Good one, Prof," Zapper said.

"Thank you, my good man." The professor was planning to write a book when he got out of this hell hole, if he did, and he liked adopting a pompous attitude from time to time. It amused him and his buddies.

For a few minutes, the group smoked in silence, finishing off the joints and lying back, each lost in the initial stage of reverie produced by Ofay's potent weed. After a while, the professor stirred and dug into his pack. He pulled out a small plastic packet containing several tiny pieces of rectangular off-white paper.

"All right." Freddy saw what the professor was up to. "Let's do it, Prof."

"You been holdin' out on us, Prof?" Ofay said.

"No way. These are the rest of those hits I got last time in Da Nang. The Air Force boys at least do one thing right."

"I don't want to do no acid out here," Bertoni said. "I'm too short."

"Everybody's too short," Zapper said.

"It's mellow." The professor took one of the squares of paper. "Windowpane, smooth. Who's got the beer?"

Zapper handed him the beer. The professor took a long pull and sighed.

"Me, now." Freddy held out his hand. "Me."

The professor carefully put a piece of paper in Freddy's palm. "Easy, Mud, it's all good." He then gave Ofay and Zapper a square each. Bertoni still didn't want one.

"You goin' straight?" Ofay said.

"Weed's okay." Bertoni said. "But that shit'll mess you up into the night. I want to see tomorrow."

"This that same stuff we did at the rear?" Zapper wondered.

"That is correct," the professor answered.

Freddy whistled. He seemed to be considering Bertoni's objections before taking the acid.

"Well?" The professor waited.

"OK." Freddy laughed crazily. Bertoni sneered at him. Freddy flipped Bertoni off.

It took about a half hour for the acid to kick in good. A quarter moon had risen above the distant tree line, and it hung in the sky, transmitting a clear, if weak, light. Freddy had decided it was jumping all over the sky. From time to time he would reach out his arms as if to catch it. He giggled a lot at his failure. Bertoni, watching the rest of the platoon, tried to calm him down. Ofay, Zapper, and the professor were each in their own worlds, wrestling perhaps with personal demons. It was a quietly powerful time. Bertoni watched over his friends, content to just be loaded, aware that at any moment the calm about them could suddenly be transformed into a hellish nightmare of war.

About an hour into the windowpane, the professor leaned over toward Bertoni and whispered something. Bertoni waved his hands.

"No way. They'll bust me."

"No way, what?" Zapper wasn't sure the voice he'd heard wasn't in his own mind. "What do you want?"

"Call it in," the professor said out loud.

"Do it," Ofay said, not knowing what "it" was, "do it, white boy." Muddy Freddy giggled and rolled around on the ground.

"I can't do it, Prof, Jesus," Bertoni argued.

"You do the L-T's voice perfect, you've done it before, do it again."

"Not an air strike, good God. I never did nothing like that."

"Make it sound good."

"God, yes," Zapper exclaimed, "yes. Fire. Napalm. Oh, God, do it."

"You mothers would owe me forever," Bertoni said, "forever."

"We will," the professor said. "Anything you want in Da Nang. Anything. On us."

"Forever," Bertoni reiterated. "Money, anything I want?"

"Yeah, yeah," everyone assented.

"But, the lieutenant...."

"We'll dust him." Zapper sniffed. "He's an FNG, man, gonna get us killed probably."

"What about Davis?" Bertoni said.

"We dust him, too," Ofay said. "He ain't worth a plug nickel as platoon leader anyway."

"Grease 'em," Freddy said with glee.

"Call it in," the professor said.

Bertoni called it in. Then they waited. Bertoni looked around a couple of times to see if Davis had heard the radio squawking, but apparently he hadn't. So they settled in and waited. It wasn't too long of a wait. Two of the last F-105s in Nam came screaming in low, the blast of their engines reaching the stoned-out group just seconds before the first blast of napalm rent the dying light of day and lit it up with rolling mountains of flame produced by the jelled gas. It was an awesome sight.

"Jesus H. Christ." Zapper marveled.

"Whoa," Ofay said, "do it, mother."

Freddy and the professor watched the fiery display in reverent silence. Bertoni saw Davis come clambering across the hill toward them.

"What's going on down there. What is happening?"

"Must be some Gooks down around the trees by the river." Bertoni tried really hard to be straight. "Fly boys are cooking 'em good."

"Who called it in?" Davis said. "There's no reports of enemy activity around here. There's nothing but villagers down there."

"VC," Zapper told him, "damned VC."

"Sappers," Ofay added.

Freddy giggled. The napalm had nearly burnt itself out now. The tree line was black and gray, only scattered fires were still going. The professor had never taken his eyes off the inferno below.

"You call this strike in, Bertoni, you stupid dopehead?" Davis growled.

"No way. How could I? I ain't authorized."

"Gimme that." Davis grabbed the radio from beside Bertoni.

"I'm the radio man."

"You ain't shit from here on in, troop."

"Damn it, Davis."

"You sonsabitches better not be responsible for this." Davis wouldn't look at Bertoni. "You're all busted down if you are. You'll do time if it's up to me. You hear me?"

"Ten-Hut." Ofay saluted in the fading light.

"You're a bunch of animals. Nothing but animals." Davis took the radio and stalked off.

"Eat it, man." Zapper picked up his M-16 and aimed it at Davis's back.

"Do it," Ofay said.

"Screw it." Zapper lowered the weapon.

"What if they did hit a village down there?" Bertoni said. "Or maybe a LRRP?"

"Whoa." The professor sat bolt upright.

"So we fry a few Zips." Zapper shrugged. "Who gives a damn."

"Ain't gonna be no LRRPs down in there," Ofay said.

"How do you know?" Bertoni said.

"LRRPs is always way the hell away from us, man," Ofay said.

"It's bad karma, man," the professor said.

"Fuck karma," Zapper said, "whatever the hell that is."

"It's like whatever you do comes back—" the professor began.

"Here they come again." Freddy squealed as the 105s roared across the valley for a final drop.

Bertoni climbed away from the others. "Why did we...."

Because so little of the sun's light remained, the second drop was even more impressive than the first. The roiling fire extended high into the air and far across the valley. The entire plain was lit up in gold, yellow, and red flames. The tumbling, burning gel made shapes, then changed, formed others, over and over and over until the fire had consumed every combustible particle in its path.

"Wow, man," Zapper said, "far out."

"Yeah," Freddy echoed, "far out."

Ofay and the professor were silent, awestruck. Bertoni kept his back to the second drop.

At the outer edges of the drop, secondary fires burned sporadically, creating odd sparkling shapes in the failing light. By the time they had all burned out, night had fallen. The moon was fully risen but put out only a weak light.

Bertoni walked further away from the others then, toward the middle of the firebase. He felt lightheaded and sick to his stomach, afraid to look back into the enclosing darkness. He had never felt less high in his life.

TIN SOLDIERS AND NIXON COMING

WHEN DANI LANE ARRIVED HOME for the Christmas Holidays during her sophomore year in college, Grandpa Gabe Bowen was already ill in bed with a high fever. Grandpa Gabe had moved in with Dani's parents the previous summer. He had done so, according to Dani's mother, Gabe's daughter, kicking and screaming.

The old man had reached the stage where he was no longer able to adequately care for himself in the house he and his wife, Dani's grandmother, gone now some five years, had lived in for three decades. Knowing that he had reached another checkpoint in the clear path of his declining years did not sit well with the highly independent old man. But now, just a few months later, with a bad flu or some kind of virus burning through his body, it was a good thing the old man had people to look out for him.

Dani, who was Gabe's favorite grandchild and knew it—her older brothers, Harry and Bill constantly reminded her should she ever forget—was happy to watch out for Grandpa. When she was young, he had often given her little presents that he didn't give the boys, always had some sort of chocolate treat for her, and would pat her on the head kindly, tousling her long, thick dark hair.

"Are you awake, Grandpa?" Dani pulled a chair alongside the old man's bed. "Mom gave me some Ibuprofen for you to take and some awful-smelling cold medicine."

"Don't want that," Gabe muttered.

"But you have to have it. We've got to get you well. It's almost Christmas. Can't have Grandpa sick for the holidays."

She handed the old man two brown pills which he dutifully swallowed with a big drink of water from a glass she held out.

"What's that other crap?"

"Some kind of cold medicine, Grandpa. Mom says it'll break up your clogged sinuses."

"It's green. Looks like it'll kill me instead of make me well."

"Don't be such a big baby."

Gabe winked at his granddaughter and managed to down the foul-smelling and tasting liquid.

"Ugh. That was horrible."

"But now it's all done."

"You'd make a great doctor, kiddo."

"Just for you, Grandpa, just for you."

"Thanks, sweetheart. Did I ever tell you you're the spitting image of your late grandma?"

"Only about a thousand times. Now lean back and rest. I'll be right here."

"You do, you know." Gabe yawned, stretching his old body in the bed.

"I know." Dani plumped up his pillow and tucked in the covers.

"I'm feeling sleepy."

"Rest then. It'll be good for you."

For a few moments, Gabe was quiet. He closed his eyes, and his breathing became slower, more shallow. Dani watched over him, waited for him to definitely fall asleep. Just as she thought he was out, he mumbled something.

"What, Grandpa?" She leaned closer to the old man to hear.

"Don't have a clue," Gabe whispered.

"Who doesn't have a clue?"

"Nobody." the old man's voice trailed off.

"Sure, no clue."

"Wrong." The old man managed to get out, just as he was falling asleep, "I was completely wrong."

"Oh, Grandpa." Dani held one of the old man's bone-skinny hands. "You're not wrong. You're the smartest man I know. You…."

But the old man was out now, far away, dreaming of another time and place. A night from his youth, one that still lived within his aged soul and always would.

———————

"GIVE ME A HIT OFF that." Gabe reached for a fat joint his good friend Pete held.

"Easy, big man." Pete handed over the doobie in question. "You don't wanna get so messed up you can't taste the food, do you?"

"Not likely." Gabe took a big hit off the joint.

It was New Year's Eve, and Gabe had joined his college buddy Pete, his girlfriend Cindy, and brother Eddie to celebrate the New Year. Pete and Eddie Avila were actually Pedro and Eduardo Avila from Chile. They had emigrated from South America to the Midwest some years back.

Pete had been drafted while still an alien, learning his English and gaining citizenship while serving in the U. S. Army in Viet Nam. Eddie, a few years older, had somehow missed the draft and was now a budding entrepreneur as well as a top-notch cook.

"How's the food comin'?" Gabe called from behind a hazy cloud of smoke.

"Almost done." Eddie gave his tantalizing paella recipe a final stirring. "Another five or ten minutes. You guys wash up, and it'll be ready."

When the food finally hit the table, Gabe made a glutton of himself, piling his plate high with the flavorful mixture of rice, crabs, chicken, shrimp, and sausage. A beer or two after the meal helped settle him down.

"You're going to explode, Gabe," Cindy teased.

"Too good not to do it." He belched loudly.

"God." Pete pretended to be offended. "You *gringos* are such pigs."

"When the revolution come." Gabe conjured up words from the Last Poets album they'd been listening to all afternoon. "You won't be calling me piggy, you'll be saluting me as Comandante Gabriel."

"Oh, my God," Eddie said. *"Díos mío."*

"Mira, *comandante."* Pete snickered. "Just because you had a little trouble back in school doesn't mean you're a revolutionary now."

"The system tried to take me down." Gabe pushed his long hair away from his face melodramatically. "And we beat it."

"That's why you can no longer live back there," Pete reminded his friend. "Because you beat it?"

"I ain't in jail, am I?"

"Fair enough."

Gabe had been told by their old college that he couldn't go to graduate school unless he "cleaned" up—that was, get a haircut, shave, and stop looking like a hippie. In addition to his unacceptable appearance, Gabe was an award-winning student journalist and had written pointed articles for the campus newspaper and a number of satirical pieces about the school administration for the student government newsletter. The two things together had apparently triggered his "dismissal" from grad school.

Not one to just step back from a good political fight, Gabe threatened to take the school to court over his expulsion. In short order, he found himself on the wrong end of a trumped-up arrest, charged with assaulting a police officer during a campus disturbance.

Only his actual innocence and the testimony of six to eight people who put him in another town during the so-called disturbance kept him from real jail time. He had won the battle but not the war. He had to move on, leave the little college town behind, at least for the time being.

"Yeah," Cindy said "let's get ready to go. The concert starts in less than an hour. We need to get with it."

"Right on, baby." Pete kissed her on the cheek. "It's time for dessert now."

"I couldn't eat another bite," Gabe said.

"No, man," Pete said, "it's a whole other kind of treat."

"What are you talkin' about, dude?"

"Show him, sweetie," Cindy said.

"What are you guys up to?"

Pete opened his hand and held it out for the others to see. There were five small pills in his palm.

"Acid?" Joanie guessed.

"Naw, man, this is supposed to be pure THC. The heart of the cannabis, man, brought right down to its essence, you dig?"

"Oh, I dig." Gabe said.

He'd never heard of such a thing, but he was ready for it. Back in school one time, they had tried to make hash by boiling down weed in a big pot. All they got was a ruined pot and some sticky residue on the bottom. The scientific experiment had failed the unscientific group. If this stuff was what Pete said it was, it would be way stronger than hash. The thought made Gabe shiver like he'd already gone out into the cold New Year's Eve night. It didn't stop him from downing one of the pills with a big chug of beer, however—nor any of the others either.

"Well," Pete said, when everyone had swallowed one of the pills, "here we go."

THE DRIVE TO THE CONCERT arena was uneventful, with the exception of more weed smoking and Eddie's inability to remember where they were going or for what reason.

"We're going to see Rare Earth, dude," Pete reminded his brother several times. "Downtown. The big concert place, man."

"Yeah," Eddie snickered each time Pete retold him. "Dig it, Rare Earth."

The whole group was giggling by the time they got to the arena, and it was virtually miraculous that they found the ticket line and got into the show.

Walking into the big music hall, with three levels of seating rising up from the floor in front of the stage, Gabe realized that whatever they had dropped—pure THC or some garden variety of LSD, it didn't really matter at this point—was really kicking in. Canned music was playing and weaving in and out of his brain as if moving from side to side. He could hear the hum of the crowd and bits and pieces of hundreds of conversations going on in the buzzing throng.

He figured there must have been eight or ten thousand in the arena or convention center or wherever it was that they were. It was really filling up fast, and you could feel the excitement of the crowd. It was practically a physical entity it was so charged.

The friends finally found their seats and began to settle in on the second level almost directly in front of the stage. Good location, Gabe allowed. Taking off his coat, he realized he was getting so out there, so high, that he might have to rein himself in, if possible. It was warm inside after the cold outdoors, and that made him comfortable and relaxed.

He shut his eyes and listened to the sounds. Flashes of bright light shot through the space between his eyes and his closed eyelids. He felt himself drifting, floating, fading in and out of the world with the changing volume of the music, which was now blending together with the sounds of the crowd to make a mix that was both specific and undifferentiated all at the same time.

For several moments more, he kept his eyes closed, marveling at the wonderful mixture of music and human voices. He felt that free-floating sensation again, and this time it frightened him. He was getting too far out, too far from the physical reality of the arena.

Taking a deep breath, he forced his eyes open and tried to focus on his surroundings. No one seemed to have noticed that he had gone away from them, and when he looked around the arena he was suddenly overwhelmed by the size of the crowd and—more than that—who they were.

Everywhere he looked were young freaks, all younger than himself, all coming of age during this wonderful time. And he was one of them, older yes, like an older brother, sure, but one with them all. They would continue the movement, lead it to the next stage, bring on the great change that everyone so hoped for.

He had never in his life felt so connected to people, to a time, to a possibility of a greater world. And behind this feeling he heard the music that was playing as a prelude to the concert.

"Tin soldiers and Nixon coming," he heard the band playing, "we're finally on our own."

With the music and the crowd and the charged atmosphere so vibrant around him, Gabe closed his eyes again and let the powerful sense of hope he was feeling consume him, course throughout his body. And when he opened his eyes once more, he realized—strangely enough—that he was actually crying. Not loudly but weeping softly, thinking of the four dead in Ohio and how the generation had rallied around their killings. He envisioned a world beyond Kent State then, one in which such a horrific thing could never occur again. He saw an America that was just and fair and for all people, all of us.

And then that moment was gone. He hid his face so no one could see he'd gotten so emotional, and he cheered loudly when the canned music ended and the lights went down for the beginning of the Rare Earth show. He forced himself to focus entirely on the music, on his friends, on the here and now. Once he thought Pete might have had an idea what was going on with him, but he didn't look over, and then that feeling passed, too. With a raucous opening number, Rare Earth ripped into their show and all was forgotten save the concert. It was New Year's Eve—it was going to be a great time.

GABE STRUGGLED TO AWAKEN. HIS head hurt, and he felt tired, drained of energy. Still, he twisted and turned in bed. The sheets seemed awfully cold.

"Grandpa." Dani called to him. "Wake up. You're having a bad dream."

"What? I feel clammy."

"I think your fever broke. I think you're gonna beat the flu."

"Oh."

"You were talkin' to beat the band, Grandpa."

Gabe essayed a weak smile for Dani. She was a sweet child and actually seemed to care for the old curmudgeon.

"What was I saying?"

"Something about somebody being all wrong. Do you remember having a dream?"

"Not so much a dream as an old, almost-forgotten memory."

"Back in the day?"

"Yeah, back in the day."

"Was it a bad memory? Was that why it was wrong?"

"No." Gabe took a drink of water from a small glass Dani offered him. "It was a good memory. It was just that I was wrong about what it meant."

"I don't think I understand exactly. Is it a sixties kind of thing?" Gabe reached out and held his granddaughter's hand briefly.

"Yes. I thought—a lot of us thought—that something big was getting ready to happen. That the world was going to change in a really profound, positive way. But it didn't. We failed it, ourselves, everyone, and we were wrong."

"Now, Grandpa, you always tell me it's all out there in front of us and to not get hung up on the past. Always keep going forward, do the best you can every day, make something good happen today and tomorrow. Stay positive."

"You've been listening to me too much."

"No way. Just because the world didn't change like your generation thought it was going to doesn't mean my generation has to give up hope that we can make the world a better place for the generations after us."

"You're tops, kiddo. You're our—no, *the*—hope. And you're proof that just maybe we weren't totally wrong after all."

"You bet, Grandpa. That's the spirit. Never give up."

"Don't tell your folks about these conversations we have. They'll think I'm trying to turn you into a radical or something. They're a lot more conservative than you and I are. They're sticks in the mud."

"I won't Grandpa. I know."

"I know you do. That's why I can still have hope. Always keep it out there in front of you."

"That's the ticket."

"I better rest a little now, hon." Gabe rolled over on his side toward Dani. "Maybe I'll feel better after a little more rest."

"Of course you will."

Gabe closed his eyes and felt a restful, needed sleep coming on. As he drifted off, he could feel Dani placing an extra-large towel against his back and legs to cover him from the damp sheets. In seconds he was sound asleep.

The girl stayed with him then, patting his long, skinny hands and listening to him breathe slowly but steadily for another quarter of an hour. When she was sure he was okay and resting comfortably, she got up and went back out into the living room.

The family Christmas tree was loaded down with red, green, and gold bulbs and strung with silver icicles. The multicolored lights flashed off and on. It was another holiday season—a festive, hopeful time of the year.

Dani was glad her folks were out of the house for the time being. The empty quiet room seemed to match her reflective mood. In no time, she thought, it would be New Year's and another beginning. Another set of possibilities. Grandpa Gabe was at least right about one thing. It really was all out there, up ahead, out there in a future that beckoned to her, to all of us.

NORTH AMERICAN

DOS CABOS LOOKED ITS USUAL tranquil self to Todd Hartman as he guided his father's fishing yacht through the deep-water channel separating the island's interior harbor from the open sea. He was glad to be back. Venezuela had been a good time, but it was always better at home, especially on Dos Cabos, back in Wilson City, the island's only town.

A few hundred feet from the dock, he cut back on the engine, letting the big boat slowly roll in. Steering skillfully, he swung it around and brought it alongside the dock with a soft bump. Shutting the engine off, he then tied and secured the ropes to the dock.

With the boat settled in, he went below to get his things. As he was stuffing a laundry bag with soiled clothes, he thought he heard some noise above deck. He looked out a port window but could see nothing. Tossing the laundry bag in a corner, he then went to an aft closet and pulled out a three-quarters full plastic trash bag. Dragging it to the middle of the room he heard sounds again. He was sure somebody was messing around up top now. Grabbing a large flashlight for a weapon, he headed toward the stairs. Suddenly there was a loud rustling and several armed men burst in.

"What the—" His words were cut short by a rifle butt to the solar plexus.

He went flying backwards, gasping for air. He landed flat on his back beside the big trash bag, the flashlight—knocked loose from his hand—crashed against the back wall into a dozen pieces.

"Get up." A thick, square-jawed man pointed an M-16 rifle at him. "On your feet."

"This looks like it's probably it." Another of the men, a tall, skinny one, tugged on the strings of the trash bag until it opened.

Pulling himself upright, Todd watched in horror as the tall man reached into the bag and pulled out a handful of what looked like weeds or alfalfa.

"Bingo, jackpot."

Todd closed his eyes and wished he were somewhere else. Venezuela. Anywhere. He couldn't believe this had happened. He didn't know what to do. He was scared to death.

"You're under arrest, son." The burly man flashed a police ID. "This is the end of the line. Your papa will have to work to get you out of this one, that's for sure."

Todd held his head in his hands and stared at the floor. The tall man read him his rights while the rest of the cops ransacked the boat. They found nothing else. Then they handcuffed him and led him off the boat. A small crowd watched as the arresting force, their suspect and contraband in hand, marched off the dock and to their cars for the brief ride to Wilson City's tiny, uncomfortable jail.

"BUENAS TARDES." TODD CALLED INTO the Benitez home. "Is Gloria home?"

Mrs. Benitez opened the door, her face an impassive mask. A boy, about twelve, tried to shove in beside her. She frowned at him.

"Hola, Todd," the boy said happily.

"Hola, 'Fredo."

"Alfredo!" Mrs. Benitez pushed the boy back. "Get out of the way."

"*Adios,* Todd."

"Bye, 'Fredo. See you later." The boy disappeared into the darkness of the house.

Todd looked up to see an even darker frown on Mrs. Benitez's face than the one she had for little 'Fredo. "Please, *Señora.* I need to see Gloria."

"No." She started to shut the door.

"Mrs. Benitez, please."

"No. She does not want to see you."

"Doesn't want to see me?"

"No. I'm sorry."

"Mrs. Benitez, just for a moment."

"No, goodbye."

"Mrs. B...."

"I'm sorry, no." Mrs. Benitez shut the door firmly.

Todd went around to the side of the house, making sure she couldn't see him. He reached Gloria's room and looked in the window. She was talking to little Alfredo and didn't see him. Todd tapped lightly on the window. He watched Gloria stop Alfredo from running to him. She pointed, and Alfredo, head down, obediently left the room. When he was gone, Gloria came to the window and opened it.

"You've got to stop coming. If my father or Frankie see you, we'll both be sorry."

"I'm sorry, Gloria, I had to see you. You and 'Fredo are all I have left. Everyone else treats me like dirt now."

"You did wrong."

"But not to anyone here on the island."

"That's not how they think. What you did was wrong. You're bad."

"Is that how you feel, too? I'm bad?"

"No. But you did wrong."

Todd came closer to the window, reached up and took Gloria by the arm.

"I'm sorry. I made a mistake, but I still care for you. That doesn't have to change does it?"

Gloria put her hand on his cheek. He reached for her. She bent down, and they kissed.

"Forgive me?"

"Yes." They kissed again. "I just want things to be as they were. Before."

"They will be. You'll see. I'm going to make it so. Tomorrow I'm going to play on the baseball team again. I don't care what the others say, I'm going to play. This is my home, too. My friends."

"No, no, Todd, don't. Please. Francisco said if he sees you near me or at the games, he'll beat you up."

"Me and Frankie fight? We're like brothers."

"He's angry, Todd. He means it."

"It'll pass."

"Maybe, but please don't go tomorrow."

All of a sudden, little Alfredo ran breathlessly into Gloria's room.

"Mama...." was all the warning he could get out. "Mama."

"Go. Now, please." Gloria shut the window quickly and with a wave turned and hurried toward her bedroom door, Alfredo closely in tow.

Todd watched as they went out of the bedroom and into the main part of the house. He stood there for a while and then with a sigh headed back to his motorbike.

———————

TODD'S OLD TEAM WAS WARMING up alongside the ball field when he arrived. He saw Gloria and Alfredo in the stands, but there was no sign of their parents. He was glad about that. He waved to them with his glove. They waved back but he could see, even from a distance, the worried look on Gloria's face.

"Mando. Teo." Todd approached some of his teammates playing catch. "Seen Francisco?"

One of the men looked in the direction of a tin-roofed, makeshift dugout on the near, first base side of the field. Todd followed the man's eyes.

He saw Frankie neatly stacking a row of wooden bats. Just before Todd reached the gap in the fence giving access to the field, Frankie saw him. He ran toward Todd. In the stands, Gloria saw them and started down the bleachers toward the field. Frankie was quickly face to face with Todd.

"What do you want here?"

"I'm the left fielder, remember?" Todd said.

"Not anymore."

"What? Come on, Frankie. What's going on here? Why are you doing this to me? We're friends."

"I'm not doing anything to you. You're off the team. That's all."

"Why?"

"You know why."

"That's between me and the courts, Frankie. I didn't do anything to you or to anyone else."

"That's not how it is here." Gloria, Alfredo, and several others formed a small group around the antagonists. "Dos Cabos is not like that. It's not some drug port for rich Americans like you."

"Lighten up."

"And stay away from my sister and little brother." Frankie put a thick forefinger against Todd's chest. "I know you've been to my house. From now on, keep away."

"Stop it, Francisco." Gloria stepped in between her brother and Todd. "Stop it this instant."

Todd reached for Gloria to move her out of the way. Frankie exploded, grabbing Todd by the shirt and causing him to bump into Gloria. She cried out, and little Alfredo ran to his sister's side.

"Never touch my sister again." Frankie shoved Todd backwards, away from Gloria.

Todd pushed back, and then Frankie hit him. The punch, a straight right, caught Todd flush on the chin and knocked him down. Gloria struck out at Frankie until he had to restrain her.

"Damn you, what's the matter with you, with all you people?" Todd picked himself up. "You act like judge and jury on everyone's life. You have no right."

"We have the right," Frankie said.

Todd held up a hand indicating he wanted no more fighting. Gloria went to Todd. Alfredo stood to one side, terrified. Frankie cooled a little.

"It's best you stay away, Todd, maybe better you should leave."

"You're wrong, Frankie." Todd rubbed his aching jaw. "All of you are. I made a mistake, and I'm sorry. I can't change it, but I didn't mean to hurt anyone on Dos Cabos."

"You know how it is here. You knew when you came here. You're like all the other *yanquis*. You think you can do anything and get away with it. You think the judge should treat you better because you're an Anglo. And he will. We're proud people on Dos Cabos, and we don't want your kind around. Goodbye."

Frankie picked up Todd's glove where it had fallen in the dirt and tossed it to him, then turned and walked back to the dugout. Todd stood watching him for a moment, without speaking to Gloria or Alfredo, then he walked away, too.

Gloria and the boy followed, calling for Todd to wait. But he just kept going. At the edge of the dirt parking lot he passed a garbage can and, pausing, lifted the lid on the can and threw the glove in, spitting after it. He climbed on his motorbike angrily, kick started it, and pulled away from the field, dust and rocks kicking up behind.

Gloria, the boy holding onto her waist, watched Todd ride off. She cried without sound, petting Alfredo's soft brown hair. Behind them, the ball game had begun. There was the sound of wood on horsehide, and the small crowd cheered. Gloria and the boy walked away, away from the game.

From his position in the field, Frankie saw them leaving. There was nothing he could do. He was in the middle of the game now. He couldn't quit. That wasn't the way it worked. You had to go by the way things were. There was nothing else for it. Any man knew that.

INDEPENDENTISTA

ESTHER FELT PARTICULARLY AGGRESSIVE, EVEN a bit bellicose. She and the eight other members of the central committee of Boca Tierra's small but militantly vocal Independence Party—including her ex-husband Guillermo—had had a turbulent meeting. She had railed at the committee chairman, calling him a reactionary and a petty bureaucrat. Guillermo had played the reconciler among the committee, and in the end all the ruffled feathers were smoothed. After the meeting he gently chastised Esther.

"It's not us who are the enemy. You have to keep this in mind."

"Ave María. Please, Guillermo, drop the subject."

"The elections are next month. How we do in those is much more important than these little squabbles among ourselves. To gain support of the people we must set aside our internal differences and present a unified front."

"Like always you presume to lecture me. Don't."

"You know what I mean, Esther. It wasn't personal. You know the difficulties we face with the Populares and the police. They're always looking to discredit us. They'll do anything to ensure that they win. And that we lose. Anything. You know that."

"Yes. You forget I was there when they shot Miguel, no?"

"Of course I haven't forgotten. All the more reason why we should be unified. And why we should be vigilant and cautious."

"I'm not going to let them rule my life with fear."

"It's not cowardice to be careful."

"Okay, let's forget it for now. We know how we differ on things."

"Very well, you're right. I know you know best about your life."

"Thank you." Esther searched for her car keys in the frayed purse she always carried.

"Can I walk you to your car?"

"Oh, I forgot my car is at the mechanic's shop."

"I'll give you a ride."

"No problems. None of the old things?"

"No," Guillermo promised, "just a ride."

"Okay."

———————————

ON THE WAY TO THE mechanic, they were uncomfortable together, even uneasy. All the old reasons for their divorce were still there, alive, palpable, just below the surface. They tried to avoid digging them up. Guillermo asked about the children.

"They're both fine. They have all they need."

"Of course. But do you take precautions with them?"

It was always dangerous for the children of opposition leaders in a place like San Sebastian. Guillermo worried about little Carla and ten-year-old Alberto. Especially since Esther had become well known for speaking out against the Populares on television. Guillermo sometimes wondered if she thought about the dangers when she was so outspoken.

"Don't start that again, Guillermo, we've been over everything too many times already."

"They're my children, too."

"Only in name."

"Esther."

"Watch the road," she said.

Guillermo concentrated again on driving. She was so hard but so pretty. And so important to the cause. She was really only hard because of them, of what happened to them. He didn't have her energy, her commitment.

"I'm sorry, Esther. I just worry about you and the children."

"We're fine, Guillermo." Most of the toughness gone from her voice. "Really."

Guillermo took his right hand from the wheel and tentatively reached toward Esther. He pulled back before he touched her. She acted as if she hadn't seen him. He drove on.

IT WAS AFTER NINE WHEN they got to the mechanic shop, and Esther was in a hurry to pick up the children at the sitter's. Guillermo waited while she paid the bill, and the car was brought out.

"Is it running okay?" He leaned against the door of her idling car.

"Yes, it's fine."

"Then I'll see you later. Maybe tomorrow?"

"Maybe."

Guillermo sighed and turned away. Esther watched him in the rearview mirror as he walked back to his car and got in. With a small wave, she signaled him goodbye and pulled out into the busy San Sebastian traffic.

As she drove, Esther thought of Guillermo and how they had once been so young and so in love with each other. They had gone to all the protests at the university together, the ones back when things were so exciting, when it looked like there might be an independent future for their home island of Boca Tierra. Guillermo had been so handsome then, so fiery, and yet so gentle and considerate at the same time. It was a wonderful period for them and the country, and she still felt a thrill in recollecting it.

Before they knew it, though, it was over. The brief rebellion was crushed, and she and Guillermo were surprised to have the unexpected responsibility of an unplanned child. The exigencies of making a living came first then, and their idealism wore away. With the second child came not increased joy but more misfortune as Guillermo, feeling trapped in his life, began to drink and occasionally miss work. It was the classic modern break-up. Esther went more and more into the children and the small but growing party, Guillermo to depression and eventually another woman.

"Damn him." Esther maneuvered the car down the Jose Martí freeway.

Clearing the top of an overpass near the city's botanical gardens, she heard a loud metallic snap from underneath the car. There was a momentary free play in the steering but she was able to regain control. Probably hit something. These streets were horrible.

She continued on her way down the freeway, zipping past the bright, flashing lights of the city, subconsciously hearing its hum of life amid the whistling of tires on pavement. Coming up over the next overpass, she realized almost too late that it was her exit, and she had to shift lanes abruptly to get off the freeway. A car in the near lane honked but she ignored it.

Entering the exit at over fifty miles an hour, she pushed down with her right foot to brake the car. The brake went straight to the floor. She tried the brakes again and again, but nothing happened. The car, only slightly slowing up, began to lean heavily toward the embankment as she fought to guide it down the exit.

As the vehicle slid precariously close to the edge of the road, she turned the steering wheel sharply. It spun uselessly on the column. Now out of control, the car cleared the embankment at over forty miles an hour, spun over once in the air, and landed on its roof, the impact completely crushing and flattening the top of the car.

Police were on the scene within a quarter of an hour and proclaimed it a fatal accident caused by driver error. The car was immediately towed away by the authorities.

In his mourning, Guillermo noted with some irony that Esther's death made the ninth page of the leading San Sebastian paper.

"Local woman," the stacked headlines read, "dies in car crash. Active in island politics."

That was the last thing anyone heard of Esther's death. The party, as expected, lost badly in the elections. The Populares continued in power. Guillermo, sober and withdrawn from the party, looked after the children.

ONE DAY IN THE ZOCALO

THE *FLECHA AMARILLA* FIRST CLASS bus from Cuernavaca rumbled into the south terminal in Mexico City around eight in the evening. It was too late for Evan Briggs to do much more than catch a taxi to the Hotel Monte Carlo near the *zocalo,* or city center, and grab a quick bite to eat at a nearby *taquería* before coming back in for the night.

The Monte Carlo was his favorite hotel in the city. There were other finer hotels, some even closer to the *zocalo,* and there were even less expensive ones, but the Monte Carlo had reasonable rates, too, and he preferred to stay there when he came to town.

In a past life, the hotel had actually been the temporary residence of D. H. Lawrence when he was on one of his trips in search of a climate that might ameliorate his oncoming tuberculosis. Evan loved the place for its connection, short and slim though it may have been, to a true literary giant.

Later, Lawrence's one-time home had been carved up into rooms, some with private baths and some less expensive ones with shared facilities. There was even a room on top of the hotel, out on the roof, where Evan stayed once when he had arrived after ten p.m. and the Monte Carlo was fully booked.

This night, after eating at the *taquería* down the block, he considered watching television in the hotel's day room before going to bed. There were three irregular rows of chairs in front of the TV set, enough for maybe seven or eight people, and an old couch at the back for the more comfort-inclined.

There was a young woman seated in the front row, and Evan thought about maybe speaking to her, but before he could do so, the lobby was suddenly overflowing with a late-partying, raucous group of Italian tourists. With a wistful last glance at the young woman, he took the arrival of the Italians as a sign to move on and so climbed the stairs up to his room and simply went to bed.

Next morning, when he came downstairs to drop off the room key at the main desk before going out, he stopped to visit briefly with the hotel's day manager. The manager was a large man, tall, getting heavy but well-dressed and dignified. Evan enjoyed talking to him because he was the first person he had ever heard speak Castilian Spanish, using the "th" sound so essential to that way of speaking.

"*Buenoth, diath, theñor.*" The manager greeted him.

"*Buenos días,*" he replied, delighted by the man's extraordinary pronunciation of the language.

"*Habitathión, doth, veinte thiete?*"

"*Sí, señor.*" Evan repeated in his own English-accented, Mexican Spanish. "*Habitación, dos, veinte siete.* Room 227."

The man took the key, and after a few more pleasantries, which stretched Evan's Spanish toward its conversational limit, the manager placed the key in its numbered slot in the maze of cubbyholes behind the desk.

Evan headed out then for a day on the town. He decided to head over to the *zocalo* and re-familiarize himself with the area and its attractions. He came into the area, which in many respects was the heart of Mexico City—at least historically so, from the southwest. To his right, looking across the massive concrete plaza that was the square-shaped city center proper, the east side was dominated by the National Palace.

The National Palace contained the former seats of the Mexican legislature, the Chamber of Deputies, the extraordinary murals of Diego

Rivera, and the offices of the Mexican president. It was in these offices in the 1930s that Lazaro Cardenas, the country's most beloved president, save Benito Juarez, would personally greet peasants, priests, and power brokers from all over the nation.

Beside the National Palace, to the north, were the ruins of the *Templo Mayor* where hearts uncountable were sacrificed to keep the sun revolving in its orbit. Lost for centuries, the *Templo Mayor,* center of the shining Aztec capitol of *Tenochtitlan*, was accidentally rediscovered in 1978 by workmen creating the subway system in the area.

On the north side of the *zocalo* was the National Cathedral, its twin-towered bell-topped stone structure anchoring the main plaza like the giant holy monolith that it was. Within its ornate interior were enough altars, chapels, and statuaries to sate the thirst of the driest spiritual pilgrim.

On the immediate right, the south side, was a rather nondescript city government building. Just east of the building, however, to the south of the National Palace was a breezeway where musicians often gathered to play Mexican and sometimes Andean music, the latter one of Evan's particular favorites. He had been here one Christmas, too, when the streets just beyond this area were awash with countless shoppers bargaining at dozens of hastily erected vendor stalls set up to take economic advantage of the season of good will.

Back on the west side, past the open-air restaurants and jewelry stores, was the National Pawn Shop, which sat just off the plaza on the northwest corner across from the National Cathedral. Here you could see mostly unredeemable gems and jewelry but also view works of art and antiques in the building's museums. Poor and middle-class Mexicans with some sort of collateral used the National Pawn shop to float loans when they were denied elsewhere.

Passing by the building early on his morning walkabout, Evan peered in the windows at shining rings, necklaces, and other glistening valuables but walked on to the corner and then jogged across the street onto the giant concrete central plaza itself. Keeping up a leisurely pace that would take him just in front of the National Cathedral, he noticed there was quite a bit of activity going on. Maybe not as much as at Christmas time but a much larger than usual gathering for the *zocalo*.

Out in front of the cathedral, and a bit toward the west side of the plaza, was a hastily thrown together collection of small tents—almost like a city version of a campout. There were hundreds of people gathering in this area. A sign above one of the white tents read Motel 5 *Estrellas de Cancun*—Five-Star Motel of Cancun. Whoever these people were, they had a sense of humor.

Beyond the cathedral, he angled to the left, away from the National Palace and toward the ruins of the *Templo Mayor* on the northeast corner. He stood outside the temple and admired the reconstruction work—both here and at the great ruins of *Teotihuacan*, you could tell rebuilt sections by the dark rock with white inlays that had been used to reproduce the great buildings ravaged by time, the elements, and Spanish attempts to destroy all things non-Catholic.

Given all that, the *Templo* still carried the dark power of its gluttonous appetite for human sacrifice, and the thought of so many people having their chests slit open and their hearts ripped from their bodies made the hair stand up on the back of Evan's neck. He stood there looking at the great temple for a few moments then decided to walk back to the National Palace to check out the Diego Rivera murals adorning the walls of the government building.

In the interior courtyard, he turned left and took the stairway leading to the second floor. The steps led up to a landing where the stairway continued on the left and right side. The huge, colorful murals filled the center and side walls to the ceiling with depictions of Mexican history and culture through the ages.

At the top of the middle mural, he easily identified Emiliano Zapata, but many of the other figures were outside his ken. As he always did, he took the left stairway first so he could see Rivera's depiction of Frida Kahlo, the great muralist's wife, with a Red Star on her chest.

Retracing his steps, then, he took the right stairway past countless more scenes and historical figures and walked up to the second floor. He had to see the mural at the back of the floor in which Rivera depicted Hernan Cortés as a sickly green, practically alien figure whose arrival in Mexico signaled the end of the Aztec Empire and the onset of the Spanish Conquest. Evan didn't quite share Rivera's animosity to Cortés, but he did consider the Spaniard, while certainly brave, to be one of the luckiest and most destructive of the great Conquistadors.

Having satisfied his desire to reacquaint himself with the tourist side of the *zocalo,* he headed back downstairs out of the National Palace and into the open air of the great city center.

"Holy cow," he said out loud, surprised.

In the time he had been preoccupied with the *Templo Mayor* and the National Palace, the area had become absolutely filled with a mass of noisy, moving, almost swirling humanity. Across the plaza, the demonstration had grown to almost epic proportions. There were groups of people swaying back and forth everywhere, and he could hear several bullhorns competing for their attention. He was just about to head toward the demonstration when something to his right caught his eye.

A smaller crowd had gathered near a fountain whose interior was a miniature replica of *Tenochtítlan.* The imitation Aztec capitol was all in green, not like the bright colors of the one he had seen in the Anthropology Museum in Chapultepec Park, but it was impressive nonetheless. Back to the left of the fountain was what had attracted this group of people.

It was a little boy, maybe ten years old. He was dressed like a *campesino* in jeans, work shirt, red bandanna around his neck, and wearing a little straw field hand's hat. He held a child's guitar, while a man, who must have been his father, egged him into playing and singing grown-up Ranchero songs. The crowd oohed and aahed and cheered with gusto.

Evan listened to a couple of songs, joining in the general approbation of the child's talent, and was about to move along when he chanced to look over almost directly across from where he stood. There was an older woman there eating something from a white Styrofoam cup. The woman held the cup tightly and close to her face as she took bites from whatever it was. Because of the woman's odd body language, Evan focused on the cup, tried to see what it was she was snacking on.

"Whoa. Chicken feet. She's eating chicken feet."

He stared at the woman, entertained by her possessive control of the cup of chicken digits—a delicacy he'd heard about but never seen. As his interest in the odd scene was about to run its natural course, the woman saw him looking at her. Her eyes widened, and she made a jerky motion, pulling the cup and its precious contents toward her body, away from the prying eyes of the foreigner across from her.

Evan turned his head away, not wishing to offend the woman, nor frighten her by thinking he was interested in the cup of chicken feet. He imagined she believed that any moment he would make a mad dash to steal those bony yellow fowl fingers from her Styrofoam cup. Shaking his head and smiling, he walked away from that crowd and headed toward the much larger one at the bottom center of the *zocalo*.

In not much more than a heartbeat, he was smack in the middle of hundreds, perhaps thousands of protestors. There were signs everywhere and innumerable smaller collections of people in various stages of debate. He read several of the signs in an attempt to gain some understanding of what was going on. Apparently, the demonstration had to do with government aid, or the lack thereof, to farmer groups throughout the country.

For a few moments he chatted with a friendly-looking *campesino,* but Evan's Spanish wasn't good enough to understand much more than that the man was looking for donations for his farm workers' union. He dug a few low denomination *peso* bills out of his pocket and handed them over.

"*Gracias, señor,*" the friendly campesino said. "*Muchisimas gracias.*"

"*De nada.*" Evan didn't mind giving a few pesos for the cause.

Angling toward the southwest corner of the *zocalo,* the one closest to the Monte Carlo and the one from which he had entered, he stopped by a vendor selling tiny Mexican flags. Given the way things were going there in the plaza, he thought a bit of Mexican nationalism was not inappropriate for a visiting North American. He bought two of the little flags and unfurled them.

As he neared the corner, there was a sudden surge in the crowd and a shift in its previously benign, if somewhat raucous, atmosphere. The crowd was building, almost by the minute it seemed, and the sound level was increasing in direct proportion to its growing size. Things seemed to be getting a bit out of control, and he was jostled back and forth by the now swirling mass of humanity.

"Time to start heading back." The sound of his own voice was lost in the noise of the rumbling throng around him.

Clutching the little Mexican flags, he tried to weave through the demonstrators without bumping into anyone too hard. Even at that, he was forced to occasionally push his way toward the corner to avoid being fully swept up in the swaying, swirling motion of the huge mass of people filling the *zocalo* from top to bottom and side to side.

At last he reached the street corner on the southern edge of the plaza, just a short block from the quieter, gentler streets leading back to the Monte Carlo. The crowd around him continued to grow, become more boisterous, more threatening in a generalized way. He waited there while people and automobiles filled the street—so much so, that there was a virtual gridlock of humans and vehicles.

To his left, he saw a policeman arrive and clamber out of his patrol car, but the officer had no chance to control what was going on now. Just to Evan's right, a portion of the demonstrators were becoming active. They chanted slogans, pumped their fists in the air, and then, without warning, began rocking a private car that had gotten too far past the intersection.

"Whoa." His words were once again lost in the swelling roar of the nearby crowd. "I'm outta here."

The protestors kept bouncing the car from side to side, getting it dangerously close to tipping over. Evan decided to make his move to safety.

Waving the little Mexican flags in a showy display of patriotism by a rank foreigner, he hurried through the throng shouting *"Viva Mexico!"* and moved as quickly as he could past the thickest part of the crowd. The fate of the car, the demonstrators, and the lone policeman was lost on him—he never looked back.

At the next intersection, he turned left and hustled on down to *Calle Uruguay.* The Monte Carlo was only a couple of blocks away and would be extremely peaceful after the excitement of the *zocalo.* That would be just fine with him today. He looked forward to the old-world tranquility of the hotel.

Maybe the entertaining Castilian-speaking manager would still be on duty, or maybe he would just sit quietly in the day room and watch some horrible *telenovelas* on the TV. He looked forward to just relaxing a while. Heck, he wouldn't even care if the loud bunch of Italians showed up again. It was all good back here in D. H. Lawrence's old home. Safe, comfortable, away from the intensity of Mexico City's always active streets. That was the drawing card of the Monte Carlo. It was what he came for, it was where he always stayed.

CHRISTMAS IN MAZATLAN

DAVID KEARNS STOOD ON THE small balcony of his second floor hotel room staring at the sea wall across the street. Avoiding the newer area of town, where the big beachfront establishments catered to weekend tourists and college students, he had checked into Las Palmas, a cheap, slowly decaying hotel in the old part of Mazatlan. Now, with the dark of Christmas Eve approaching, he was alone waiting for a phone call.

Feeling an unexpected chill, he walked back inside and sat in a chair beside his small bed. His backpack lay by the pillow, and he reached inside it to pluck out a hand-made wooden chocolate stirrer, the elaborately carved kind that locals used in the creation of molé sauce which spiced up many Mexican food dishes. He had bought the stirrer for Suzie. Suzie, for whose call he waited. Suzie, the beautiful blonde Austrian and his constant companion during the last two weeks of study at the Academia Linguistica in Guadalajara. He checked his cell phone. He had bars. He could get it if she called.

"I'll call you, Christmas Eve." She had promised at the Guadalajara Train Station. "It'll be my present."

"Will you meet me there after?"

"You know I want to."

"Promise?"

"You'd better go. The train is loading."

He checked his phone again. The battery was charged. He tucked the phone into his shirt pocket and went downstairs.

"*Tuvo, er, tuve una llamada telefonica?*" He stumbled through bad Spanish to the desk clerk. Maybe Suzie had called the desk instead of his cell. He had left her a message where she was staying.

"No, *señor.*" The clerk replied in English. "No phone calls."

"*Gracias.*"

"*Por nada. Feliz Navidades.*"

"Merry Christmas, to you, too."

He decided to take a walk while he waited for Suzie's call. A block or two from the hotel, he found a liquor store and bought a bottle of wine to have later. Looking at the bottle made him think of her again and the fun they'd had in Guadalajara—walking arm and arm around the little plaza near their language school on Sunday nights, dancing in a local bar all one glorious evening, joking in the streets about the ubiquitous Mariachi bands.

Suzie was twenty-one, small, energetic, full of life, and revelled in her uninhibited European ways. She spoke perfect English, worked as a paralegal in Vienna, and belonged to rock-and-roll dance clubs there. David was completely captivated. But there had been competition.

There were her Austrian friends—always around, always taking her here and there. And then there was this Jim guy, an American who showed up late at the language school. He had made a beeline for Suzie—pushing himself into the scene, making a move for her attentions. Jim had also been at the train station when David left. That was annoying.

Back in the room, he sat for a long while with his mind on hold, zoned out. As the evening wore on, he came out of his stupor and ate a snack of mixed nuts he'd bought from a vendor outside the Mazatlan train station. He went out on the balcony again. He couldn't see the sea wall anymore, but a half-moon had risen, and it cast a soft yellow light on the quiet water in the ocean beyond.

After a few minutes, he went back downstairs. Still no call. He checked his cell phone. Plenty of bars, plenty of charge. No call. About nine thirty he broke out the wine, drinking straight from the bottle. By ten thirty he was feeling it. Then the phone rang. It was Suzie.

"Merry Christmas." Her voice sounded like a tinkling holiday bell.

"Where are you?" He imagined her down in the hotel lobby playing a joke on him.

"Guadalajara," came the fantasy-shattering answer. *"I told you I'd call you Christmas Eve. Hello, Merry Christmas."*

"I'm sorry. Merry Christmas."

"That's better. Are you having fun?"

"I'm by myself. I have some wine."

"Your own Christmas present."

"Yes. Are you coming here?" There was a short pause, one that extended into a long one. "Suzie?"

"Yes?"

"Can you come out here?"

"David...." she began.

It was all he needed to hear. "Is it that Jim guy?"

"Can't we keep this fun? Like always."

"I had hoped...."

"My Austrian friends want me to go to San Miguel de Allende before we go back home."

"Is Jim going, too?"

"Yes, but that's just because he's here, David."

"I see."

"I told you I would call you tonight. It's my present to you. I promised, but it's all I can give you."

"I thought maybe you would be coming here." He glanced at the wooden stirrer resting on top of his backpack.

"I'm sorry. David, are you still there?"

"I'm here."

"I've got to go now, everyone's waiting. Please have a wonderful Christmas. Goodbye. Thank you for Guadalajara. I'll always remember it."

"Goodbye." He shut off the phone when he saw the connection was gone.

That was it, then. That was his Christmas present. A goodbye call. Sighing, he gathered himself and poured the wine down the bathroom sink. He didn't need that anymore.

Walking out on the balcony, he looked at the calm, moonlit ocean. Tomorrow was Christmas. He would give the chocolate stirrer to the first nice Mexican lady he saw and then catch the train home, be back by New Year's. He would begin life anew, go forward—without Mexico, without Suzie. There was nothing else he could do.

After a moment, he stepped back inside and closed the balcony doors. The room looked empty, barren. He would get the first train out in the morning. All he had to do was make it through the night. That was all he had to do.

TIME PIECES: THE TRIAL

INSIDE, THE PROSECUTOR'S VOICE DRONED on. Outside, a group of children played on the courthouse lawn. From his seat at the defense table, Jim Finerty heard and saw but made little sense of either. His attention was instead drawn inward, pulled there by an unsettling notion that he was a third party to his own trial—an observer, an impotent bystander.

"We've already heard considerable testimony." The prosecuting attorney aggressively reminded the overflow crowd in the little courtroom. "That the defendant has a predisposition toward antisocial behavior. His books are, as we are clearly showing, obscene."

"Your Honor." Jim's lawyer objected. "Please. The prosecution's summing up again."

"Mr. Bratz?" The judge lifted one thick eyebrow.

"Very well." Bratz—the prosecutor—wasted a sneer on Jim, who watched a bundled-up little boy kick a can across the street outside. There was a quiet pause. "If it please the court, Your Honor. We would like to call our next witness."

"The State calls Reverend Theo Tolliver to the stand." A young clerk tried to hide the excitement in her voice.

Jim noticed her for the first time. Dark, with round, substantial hips and long, fine legs. He watched her until Reverend Tolliver's grating voice brought him back to the less pleasant reality of the trial.

"My church's Clean Book Committee," Tolliver explained, "exists solely to exalt and clarify God's word and to suppress pornography and other hateful literature."

"In what way, sir?" Bratz said.

"In what way, sir?" Tolliver repeated.

"Are they obscene, for example?"

"Obscene?"

"Is there an echo in here?" Jim whispered to Tom Alton, his attorney.

"Absolutely, sir." The Reverend went on. "Mr. Finerty's books are nothing but filth. They blaspheme our nation, our free enterprise system, our democratic way of life. His books are riddled with despair, with hopelessness. In a word, they're depressing."

"Your Honor." Alton rose from the defense table with a pained smile. "Is depression to become a crime now, too?"

The audience stirred with low laughter.

"You'll get your turn, Mr. Alton." The judge lightly rapped his gavel. "Be patient."

"Well, then, Reverend Tolliver, sir." Bratz resumed. "Is there anything else you'd like to add?"

"I would like to reiterate," Tolliver said, "that Mr. Finerty has written books so vile our parish felt justified in demanding their removal from our schools and public library."

"Because of the obscenity in them?"

"Yes, sir. And because of their decidedly un-American perspective. Those are our criteria. These works flagrantly violate them both."

"Thank you, sir." Bratz said. "That's all we needed to hear. I have no other questions for you."

Reverend Tolliver started from his chair.

"Just a moment," the judge said. "Mr. Alton, any questions?"

Alton glanced at Jim, who looked away.

"No, sir." Alton told the judge. "Not just now, but we would like to reserve the right to recall the witness."

"Then you may step down for now." The judge motioned to Reverend Tolliver. Tolliver bowed gravely and left the witness stand.

As he had throughout the trial, Jim soon found himself daydreaming. His eyes strayed to the window and beyond, and he found, to his disappointment, that the little kids who had been playing outside were gone.

TUESDAY

WHILE JIM'S MIND ROAMED ONCE again, Alton called the last defense witness. It was Anna Fruehling. When Jim realized it was she, he looked up in surprise. On the stand, Anna looked quite a bit thinner than he remembered, but her face still had character. Dark and intriguing, her strong midwestern features made for a surprising down to earth handsomeness.

Beneath her simple, attractive exterior, Jim could still see why she had ultimately come between him and his ex-wife Linda. Putting on hold the myriad emotions Anna's presence and Linda's memory aroused in him, he made himself listen to Anna's version of their shared past.

"Given the nature of your prior relationship," Alton said, "do you believe you can be unbiased about Mr. Finerty and his work?"

"Yes. I think I can."

From the prosecutor's table, Bratz snorted and made a production out of shuffling his notes. Alton looked at him, then turned back to the witness.

"Miss Fruehling, as a member of the literary community could you give us, in your own words, what you think of Mr. Finerty's books?"

"That's a tough question to answer off the top of my head."

"Do the best you can."

"Quite honestly, I would say his work is probably average or maybe a bit above. Its real strength is in the organization, the subject matter, and the, uh, intent."

"Intent?"

"Yes."

"What do you mean?"

"Well, as I understand his aims, he's trying for a type of realism in his work. He once told me he thought writers should only try to record real things and real people in the specific time in which they existed."

"Miss Fruehling, given your general opinion of Mr. Finerty's work, what is it, would you say, that makes it obscene enough to put him in this courtroom today?"

"Mr. Alton, I don't believe this trial has anything to do with obscenity. It's purely political. His work directly challenges the system, the status quo. That's why we're here."

"Your Honor." Bratz objected, rising. "This witness is off on a tangent This is an obscenity trial. It has nothing to do with politics."

"Mr. Alton," the judge said, "please redirect."

"Yes, sir," Alton said, then again to Anna. "Would you characterize the defendant's work obscene?"

"If the only purpose of art is to reaffirm the current values of a society, regardless of the legitimacy of those values, and if to challenge them in literature is viewed as obscene, then I'm afraid Mr. Finerty and a lot of other writers' work is obscene."

"Thank you, Miss Fruehling. That's all I have. Counselor."

"Very nice job, Mr. Alton." Bratz rose from the prosecutor's table. "And thank you. I have only a couple of questions for your 'star' witness here."

He waved toward the stand and stood directly in front of Anna. She lowered her eyes.

"Miss Fruehling, we've heard you describe the defendant in a, uh, most positive way, but we haven't heard much about you. Let me ask you one small question, all right?" She did not look up. "Just tell everyone here your real relationship with the defendant, aren't you his lover?"

"Of course not, don't be stupid."

"Stupid, am I?" Bratz shot back fiercely. "Well, how about this? Would you say you love the defendant?"

"No—I don't know. We once had a relationship, that's all. I don't see...."

"Admit it. You're nothing more than an extension of him. You don't exist without him. You are his own creation. Isn't that right?"

"No, that's not true. He did get me started, but that was a long time ago."

"Your Honor." Alton broke in. "Mr. Bratz is badgering the witness."

"That's all, Your Honor." Bratz quickly broke off the attack. "No further questions."

He sat down with a satisfied smile. The courtroom buzzed. The judge rapped his gavel. When he had order again, he dismissed Anna and sat shaking his head, glowering at the attorneys.

"This court is in recess, and you two," he said to Alton and Bratz, "in my chambers, now."

WEDNESDAY

"LET ME ASK YOU THIS." Bratz had Jim on the stand now, defending himself. "Is there a lot of cursing and pornography in your books?"

"Well, the answer is yes or no, depending."

"Your Honor." Bratz looked impatiently at the judge.

"Be more precise, please, Mr. Finerty," the judge said. "This is a little hard to follow."

"Yes, Your Honor. My answer to 'is there a lot of cursing in my work?' is probably. People curse in real life, and they do in my stories, too. Pornography, no. I don't believe anything in my work can be described as pornographic."

"Come now, Mr. Finerty," Bratz countered. "Don't pretend to be so saintly. We know what you are, we know what you want from your writing, don't we?"

Alton edged forward in his chair at the defense table. Jim looked at Bratz with widening eyes.

"Tell the court, won't you please, Mr. Finerty," Bratz went on dramatically. "What your real intent is. Or shall I? Whether in the guise of foul language, filth, or leftist ideology, your real purpose, Mr. Finerty, is to undermine the ideals of your readers. To overthrow their values with your own twisted set of beliefs."

"Your Honor," Alton said, "I object."

"Mr. Bratz," the judge said, "control yourself. What is your point?"

"My point, Your Honor? The point? The point is that this man is charged with obscenity, and the reason his work is obscene is because it is perverse and immoral, and because he, Your Honor, is a communist."

"Objection." Alton yelled again.

"You idiot." Jim laughed.

"Order." The judge banged his gavel repeatedly to still the roaring crowd.

"That's right. Everybody knows what you are. That's why you're a nobody. That's why they all turned against you. You're not an artist. You're a lousy perverted commie. You're un-American."

"Your Honor." Alton repeated.

"I think we'd better talk, counselors," the judge said. "Chambers again. Right now."

The bailiff rushed to call the court to order for the recess, but the judge and lawyers were out of the room before he could finish his declaration.

Jim scanned the crowd quickly and recognized an anxious pair of eyes seeking contact. Anna Fruehling gave him her best concerned look. He gave her a quick wink. She was okay, he thought, maybe we could....

He failed to finish the thought, however, as Bratz and Alton suddenly and noisily reentered the room. A moment later they were followed by the judge.

"All rise." The bailiff rushed to the front of the room.

When Jim had retaken the stand and the room settled down, the judge addressed the defense.

"Mr. Alton, do you wish to examine the witness?"

"Yes, sir, I do. We would like to make just one point."

"Go ahead."

"Thank you, sir." Alton thumbed through some papers, then approached Jim. "Mr. Finerty, do you believe you have written pornography, or undermined the state, as it were?"

"Objection." Bratz demanded.

"Overruled," the judge said.

"Go ahead, Jim." Alton tilted his head at Bratz. "Tell us your side of the issue."

Jim looked over at the judge and then at Bratz. Finally he again surveyed the crowd. They were quiet, waiting.

"My only defense, the only thing that I can say on my own behalf is that I never intended to write anything that would be considered obscene. I'm not sure I know what obscene means. I just write. It's one of the things I do. If it's obscene or un-American because somebody doesn't like it or if it tells about things certain people don't want to hear, then I guess I'm guilty. But I don't believe I am. The way I see it, criticism isn't against the law. In fact, in most times and places, criticism is a duty. It's been going on in literature almost since the beginning, if not even from day one. I see my work as part of that critical tradition, that's all. It's designed to point out reality, good or bad, but not just to tear things down. It's meant to...."

His words trailed off. His point of view, even to himself, sounded shallow, didactic. He couldn't go on. After a long silence, he sighed, then looked out at the crowd.

"I just don't believe I've written anything obscene or un-American, whatever that really means."

EYES SHUT, JIM LISTENED TO Alton wrapping up the defense. He was vaguely aware that Alton was using a low key approach in presenting the final arguments.

Despite his own resolutions to the contrary, he felt, as he had all week, like an alien, like an outsider to his own life. He continued to view the trial as something unrelated to himself. Somewhere in his mental distance he heard Alton finish and saw him walk back to their table. The bailiff called "all rise," and the judge left for his chambers. Alton scooted his chair close to Jim's.

"Hey, how was it? How did I do?" Jim didn't stir. "For crying out loud, wake up. Jesus Christ."

"What?" Jim looked over glassy-eyed.

"Crap."

For the next three quarters of an hour, while the judge remained in his quarters, the courtroom buzzed with nervous anticipation. Jim doodled on a legal pad, occasionally wiping his moist palms on his dress pants. He was relieved, if not glad, when the judge at last returned with what Jim expected was the final decision on his life.

The judge briefly restated the charges and the case, and generously complimented Bratz and Alton on their preparation and presentations. Then he cleared his throat and looked at Jim, who felt most of the strength of his body dissipate.

"Will the defendant please rise?"

Jim and Alton rose together at the defense table.

"We have no desire," the judge began, "to act as an adversary of art, nor to place ourselves as judges of literary merit. Yet the gravity of the charges requires that, to some extent, we do both. Obscenity is a serious matter, whatever its guise. We cannot, therefore, ignore the charges against you, Mr. Finerty, and merely ascribe them to an ongoing artistic conflict, which, of course, in a sense is precisely the case. If we weren't in a court of law, some less potentially disastrous conclusion might be reached, one that wouldn't involve matters of punishment, punishment perhaps by incarceration. But deciding the extremes of dismissal or imprisonment is precisely the task we are expected to accomplish.

"We have heard testimony and considered the evidence," the judge said after shuffling through his papers, "and we've had light moments and grave ones, never losing sight of the seriousness of this case. It is in fact the seriousness of this case that prompts my decision, if it can be viewed as one at all. Frankly, Mr. Bratz, Mr. Alton, I'm going to do us all, I hope, a big favor."

He considered his words before going on. Some in the crowd leaned forward in their seats.

"It's my opinion that in this circumstance, the final decision should not come from me, from this court. Indeed, such a decision, with its far reaching implications, may have to be made at the highest legal level, if not by our society itself. Whatever the ultimate outcome, it's my decision to defer it at this time and to direct the case to a higher court."

There were surprised rumblings from the crowd, caught off guard in anticipation of a more concrete verdict. The judge raised his hand for silence. Then, with a benevolent smile, he simply folded the papers before him and stood up. The bailiff rushed to the front of the room.

"All rise." He called out for the last time.

"Court is adjourned," the judge said.

He turned and left for his chambers without looking back.

Several people, perhaps reporters, hurried from the room. Alton was smiling. Jim wasn't sure why.

"What happened? Did we win? Did we lose? Is this it?"

"Remember," Alton said, "even if we should have to go to a higher court, which in a case like this I seriously doubt, the high court will toss it out. You'll see. Okay?"

"Yeah. Okay."

"Think of it as a win. They're not going to pursue this again. No court wants to make a decision in a case like this."

"You mean it just lies there, hanging in the wind?"

"I tell you what," Alton said, "why don't you forget about it for a while. Take some time off. When, or if, I hear something, I'll call you. If there's going to be another trial, we'll plan the next battle then. Okay? Be happy, you're free!"

They walked out of the courtroom then, Alton with a smile, Jim with a frown. At the end of the hall, they reached the main doors and went outside. The air was much cooler than expected. Jim clearly wasn't happy with Alton's ready acceptance of the decision—or non-decision, whatever it was.

"Nothing happened at all," he said as they gained the courthouse steps. "We're right where we were to begin with."

"Listen," Alton said, "I've got to go. Come see me in a couple of weeks even if we haven't heard anything. All right?"

"Uh-huh."

"Hang in there, man. It's all good."

Alton pulled his jacket close around him and tilted up the collar. He waved at Jim and hustled down the stairs. Jim pulled his collar up as well and huddled into his jacket.

As usual, he felt that his fate remained in somebody else's hands, that the verdict, literally and figuratively, was still out. In the meantime, he could only go on as he had before—on into the murky fog of living. That was as good as it got, it was all you could do. At least that was all he knew how to do.

Taking a deep breath, he sighed loudly then crossed the street to begin the long, chilly walk home. It occurred to him again as he walked, that the struggle, the fight, the continuing trial of life probably never was over. It never could or would be. Not as long as you lived. Not until your time was finally up. Not for at least that long.

A FATHER AND SON CHOOSE SIDES

"FATHER?"

"Yes, Son."

The son was a younger man, of average height and weight, with pleasant, Semitic features and a kind countenance. His dark hair was long and curly, and it hung down to his shoulders after the old manner. The father was also Semitic but clearly of a different age. His hoary beard covered a face that could readily transform from kind to angrily vengeful and back in a flash.

"Father, it is difficult for me to choose."

"As it should be. As it should be."

"Don't we view all men as equal?"

"A commonly held notion."

"Why do we have to choose one over the other?"

"Because they want, no, insist that we do."

"But this seems like such a trivial thing to worry about."

"We have to go along with it."

"Father, what about the drowning people there in Indonesia? They had a horrible tsunami. The poor people suffer all the time."

"It can't be helped."

"And Rwanda, shouldn't we intervene and stop all the killing. I don't think ethnic cleansing is okay under any circumstance is it?"

"That," the father explained calmly, "would only interfere with their free will."

"There are millions starving—all over the world."

"Yes, of course."

"But...."

"But we have to pick a winner here," the father reiterated. "Try to concentrate."

"How can I choose when there are sixty to seventy on each side?"

"Most of them don't really believe anyway, just ignore those."

"But there are still quite a few."

"No one said it was an easy task. If it comes out uneven, choose the side with the most on it."

"Sure, that makes it a lot easier."

"You have to have to some criteria. Let's hurry along. Have you made another choice?"

"You know, Father," the son said, "why do we care about the outcome of these events? We are expending our energy on semi-literate, self-centered prima donnas when there are many, many good, decent and needy people down there."

"Well, for heaven's sake," the father boomed. "I thought that was your bag, caring about that kind of person. You were always such a softy, such a sucker for these types. It's your goody two-shoes nature."

"I don't know if that was...."

"Son, use some omniscience for a change, will you? Nothing is more important down there than that loud-mouthed, hot dog of a wide receiver making his catch. Get the hang of it. Don't you see the beauty, the absolute perfection of his ego. The other ten players on his team didn't matter. It's only about him. He doesn't care about the offensive line blocking for him, and he doesn't care about his fellow receivers nor even the quarterback himself—the one who threw him the ball. It's all about him. Can't you see that? The holocaust, the siege of Leningrad, the reign of terror in France, the killing fields of Cambodia—none of this holds a candle to the wants and needs of wide receiver boy."

"Wow, I didn't realize."

"But now you're beginning to?"

"And I'm starting to think that we are at the mercy of these... people."

"That's one in a row."

"You mean...?"

"Uh-huh." The father nodded his great, white head.

"You mean we exist only to satisfy whimsical desires of completely egocentric humans?"

"Basically."

"Then that means." The son continued the logic. "We are actually secondary to them."

"Bingo." The father was proud of his boy.

"And that we then...."

"Careful." Warned the father.

"We don't really exist except to them?"

"I'm sorry, son."

"Then my sacrifice was...."

"For nothing." The father completed the sentence.

"It was all for nothing. And we're just their invention."

"Sorry."

"Well, then," the son said, not without some petulance, "I don't want to pick any of them."

"It could be a tie." The father tilted his head to one side in thought.

"Yay!" the son said enthusiastically.

"Except." The father pointed downward. "See that big running back? He just stuck one finger in the air for us. He's thanking us."

"What for?"

"He just scored a touchdown."

"Oh. But did he do that touchdown on his own?"

"You're a little out of date." The father said. "I guess you missed the 'me' generation and all that."

"I guess so."

"Whatever. This guy scored a touchdown, but he could only do it because his ten other teammates helped him."

"He doesn't realize that?"

"They never seem to."

"Okay, fine, but why are we supposed to ignore all the problems of the world in order to choose one set of these people over another?"

"It's our job," the father said matter-of-factly. "It's the only thing we really do."

"Really? Our only real function?"

"Sure, everything else runs on its own. You know, laws of nature, the 'I Am That I Am' stuff, that overgod thing that the Romans talked about."

"Don't mention the Romans to me, please, father." The son grimaced.

"Oops, sorry. My bad. Well, anyway, except for these games, we just stay out of the way and let circumstances dictate the outcome."

"Hmnh."

"What's wrong now?"

"I don't feel so good, Father. I don't feel worthwhile."

"Well, you might as well get used to it. Eternity is a long time."

"Eternity?"

"Or at least as long as this species lasts."

"You mean they won't last forever?"

"Not even close."

"What a relief."

"Yeah, well, if you don't mind disappearing with them."

"Seems like it would be a blessing to me."

"In the meantime," the father said, "make a choice. There's a game going on down there."

"I feel better now, Father. Now that I know that it won't last so long after all."

"Me, too. Now who you taking?"

"All right, I'll take—uh, Alabama."

"Good choice." The father exulted. "I'll go that way, too. I always liked that coach they used to have. You know, the one with the plaid hat on all the time."

"Maybe that was before my time."

"Yeah. Maybe it was, maybe it was."

FROM THE VERY FACE OF THE EARTH

DORA PEARCY WORE CURLERS IN her thinning red hair, not to improve her looks—which they no longer could and definitely did not—but for the quality of the radio reception they provided. The curlers helped bring in the signals she heard with near daily regularity. Signals that were directed to her and nobody else. Signals from far away.

Sometimes when she hung her unmentionables on a clothesline she rigged between her trailer and a nearby light pole in Shady Acres Trailer Park, always keeping on guard for that nasty, bald-headed Mr. Chase from two trailers down, she could hear the transmissions perfectly. They were nice transmissions mostly but occasionally became a little naughty, particularly when they proposed personal contact—something about probes. This latter type reception, both titillating and terrifying, had begun to occur more often than she really liked to acknowledge.

She remembered when the strange, far-off sounding voices had begun. Everett, her third husband, had just passed away from some sort of gastrointestinal problem—oddly enough, her first two husbands had passed from the same cause—and the police had come to the trailer repeatedly, talking rudely to her, suggesting bad things, not treating her properly.

One hot afternoon, after the last visit from the police about Everett and after she had put her curlers on in preparation for going out to the Bingo parlor down the block—oh, Dora loved her Bingo and kind-hearted, boring Everett had left her plenty of money for playing her favorite game—that hot afternoon, she received her first transmission.

At first it wasn't clear, and she wasn't sure what was happening. The voices had been hard to understand through the static. They were high-pitched, almost childish voices. She had just given her curlers a good tap with her thumb and forefinger and went on about her business. For a few days the voices stopped. But after a visit by a not nice man from the district attorney's office, the transmissions came back loud and clear, and regularly.

When she finally got used to them, Dora found the voices to be rather comforting, mostly. They told her not to worry, that things would be okay. That she was all right. They always came to her after some troubling person or event had bothered her, and she thought that was kind of them. Right away she noticed the connection between her curlers and the signals coming in, and so the former were now seldom, if ever, out of her hair. She knew it was her link to out there, to beyond, to the mostly good stuff.

Sometimes, though, she reluctantly had to admit to herself, her contacts insisted she do certain things that were not always so good. For one thing, they suggested she invite nasty old Mr. Chase from two trailers down for dinner and cook him the same beef stew—with her special spices in it—that she had fed her late husband Everett, but Dora didn't cotton much to that idea. She mumbled "no" to the voices.

The voices had gone quiet then for several days and she began to worry they had left her for good. She apologized to them, begged their forgiveness, promised to think about feeding Mr. Chase her special stew. To her joy, the voices started up again. Louder, more excited, more demanding. They insisted on the dinner date.

Mr. Chase, of course, was thrilled to get the invitation. Dora sniffed to think how readily he did so. Mr. Chase would try to touch her somewhere bad, she was sure of that. He had a bad reputation in the trailer park. He whistled at all the women, leered at the young girls, winked at them all. She shuddered to think of what a "sicko" Mr. Chase was. But the voices insisted. Even promised they would come to her, show themselves, explain who they were. She shivered to think of how wonderful that would be, how thrilling.

The voices gave her some hints about themselves. They were not of this world, they told her, but had traveled millions of light years for the sole purpose of contacting her specifically. Although it was obvious they were vastly superior to earthlings, they assured her that all they wanted to do was introduce her to their customs, to give her knowledge of their world. They promised to take her up to their spacecraft. To show her around, maybe give her a few tests to see how earth people differed from them.

On the night of the dinner date with repulsive old Mr. Chase, the voices were so loud in Dora's head they nearly made her forget to add the special spice to the stew.

"Quiet down." She warned the voices, as she liberally sprinkled the special spice over the stew and then stirred it into the thick meaty mixture. "You almost made me mess up dinner."

"What's that?" Mr. Chase called out from the small space off the kitchen that Dora called the dining area of her old, cluttered single-wide trailer.

"Nothing." She poked her head around the corner of the narrow doorway separating the tiny kitchen from the rest of the trailer. "Nothing at all."

"Oh." Mr. Chase gave her an oily, unwanted leer.

"Disgusting." She muttered under her breath and turned back to the stew.

To pay Mr. Chase back for his leer and his general bad attitude, she tossed in another good pinch of the special spice, crying out, "Bam!" like she'd seen that cooking man do on TV.

Mr. Chase had a hearty appetite. He ate one big plate full of stew, with a large piece of buttered cornbread and then another. Dora could barely watch him without getting nauseous. Bits of food flew out of the corners of his mouth, and when he leered at her, she had to look away to keep from gagging at the sight of little pieces of meat between his yellow, crooked teeth.

As soon as he finished his third, tall glass of iced tea, she hustled his bloated self out of the trailer. Just as she knew he would, Mr. Chase tried to grab her by the door, putting his big, smelly body next to hers in a repellent attempt to hug and kiss her. She nearly had to put a knee into his unthinkables to keep him back, and she almost caused him to fall down the rusted steps of her trailer as she pushed him down and away from her.

She closed the door on his final words but heard enough to know he had high hopes of repeating the evening's event and that next time perhaps their "relationship" could move to the next level—whatever that meant. Shaking her shoulders as if a cold wind had just brushed across her bare neck and head, she snorted and pushed the door tightly closed, carefully securing and locking it.

SERGEANT RALPH HANSON MUNCHED HAPPILY, with no visible sense of irony at the police stereotype he presented to those in the restaurant around him, on a large, powdered-sugar covered donut. He and his partner Corporal Tom Atkins had stopped for coffee and a sweet treat at Jimmy's Diner, a local greasy spoon with the reputation of having the best cakes, pies, donuts, and coffee in town.

"Another cup, Corporal?" Lou Ann, one of the mainstays in Jimmy's waiting corps and its most veteran member, said.

"Not for me." Atkins covered the top of his mug with his left hand.

Hanson, smiling a powdered-sugar smile, held his cup out and wagged it up and down for Lou Ann to refill.

"You're gonna get fat as a pig." Atkins warned his partner. "Slammin' those greasy sugar bombs all day."

"You fret too much." Sergeant Hanson countered, but he did pull in his growing stomach and give it a loud swat with his left hand. Atkins could see little flakes of white appear on the sergeant's clean uniform.

"I guess so."

The corporal checked the front page of the local newspaper, *The Martinsville Monitor.*

"Says here, Ralph," who belatedly covered his mouth after a small burp, "there's going to be a big meteor shower tonight. Should be able to see it really well if the weather stays clear."

"What time?"

"From nine to eleven according to this."

"We could drive out to the dam and check it out after our shift." Hanson suggested. "Take a couple of brews. Watch the show."

"I don't know, my wife...."

"There might be flying saucers mixed in with the falling stars."

"What?" Atkins shut off an image of his wife reading him the riot act for coming in late after his shift—once again. "What are you talking about?"

"Some people think that's how they come in all the time to watch us. They mix in with these meteor showers."

"You should've never gone to Roswell that time." Atkins gave Lou Ann the waitress, who had continued to hover nearby, a wink.

"I'm just telling you," Hanson said.

"You should go hang out with that old Mrs. Pearcy out at the trailer park, then." Atkins ribbed his partner. "They say she talks to the space aliens all the time."

"I'm serious."

"So is she—uh-oh."

"What is it?"

Atkins dug into the right pocket of his uniform pants and pulled out a pager. He had put it on vibrate so as not to bother the other diners.

"We got a call."

"Let's go." Hanson rose and tossed a couple of bills on the counter by his coffee cup.

"'Night, Lou Ann." Atkins called back as the officers hurried out of the diner. "'Preciate it."

"Good night, officers. Don't take any plug nickels from them spacemen."

———————

LIGHTING AT THE SHADY ACRES Trailer Park was not good, and Dora had complained about it to the management numerous times. Tonight, however, that poor lighting was a benefit. By walking around to the back of her trailer and then past a couple of big trees, she was able to see the night's meteor shower in all its glory. She watched the streaking meteors with something like the awe she had felt when seeing a shooting star as an innocent girl, one safe from the concupiscent longings of degenerate men and the no doubt painful probings of strange off-world beings.

About forty-five minutes into the shower, just as she was beginning to think about going back inside to have a snack and maybe a small something to drink, she saw it—an especially bright meteor. It was different than the others, not just because it was much brighter, which it was, but because it was not whitish, but green, foggy green, huge, and scary close.

This meteor, fuzzy and greenish, came in slower than the others, larger, slower, apparently hitting down in a place that looked to be only a few miles outside of town. Dora expected a loud noise, an explosion, fire, something, but there was nothing. All was quiet. She wondered if others had seen the meteor, if that was what it was, and she considered calling the authorities, but her recent experiences with the police negated that option right away.

Although she was feeling a little unsettled after the big meteor came down, she stayed outside for a few minutes more, watching the sky and occasionally lifting her eyes to the horizon—like her father had taught her when she was a little girl—in order to see if there was anything moving out that way. Holding her left hand above her eyes to shield them from what little light the trailer park gave off, she watched the base of a line of trees maybe a quarter mile away.

"Oh, heavens," she squeaked.

There was movement by the trees. She checked again. Nothing at first, but then there it was again. Definite movement.

"Dear Lord."

Flinging up her arms in terror, Dora hurried for the safety of her trailer. Stumbling breathlessly up the front stairs, she fumbled at the door before finally getting it open and rushing inside. She quickly locked and bolted the door and slid the chain on. Working feverishly, she pushed a thick chair in front of the door and piled a big trashcan on top of that.

For several minutes she stood before the door, afraid to breathe, hoping against hope that she had barricaded herself in enough to stop whoever or whatever was outside. Finally, she began to relax a bit, to calm down. She exhaled slowly and backed away from the door. Just as she did there was a scratching on the window screen directly behind her in the living room. Turning slowly toward the noise, she held her arms tightly against her body as if that would protect her from any shock that might be awaiting. It didn't.

"Oh, my God." She shrieked, flinging her arms up protectively in front of her face. "Help. Help. Get away. Get away from there."

Outside, through the living room window, she could see them. Them. The ones with big, black eyes. The ones with skinny little bodies, huge heads, long spider-like arms. The ones on the covers of the tabloids down at the grocery store. The ones that were always photographed walking with whoever was the sitting president. It was them, those, the ones.

"Please, please." She moaned, her mind racing with visions of light beams taking her up into a spacecraft, of strange beings in strange settings, of unspeakable examinations on and in her body, of abductions to places far, far from the familiar world of Shady Acres Trailer Park.

"Help." She moaned again, just before her eyes glazed over and she fell face-first onto the couch beneath the living room window, face-first onto the scratchy, cloth surface of the couch, face-first—completely unconscious.

"WHOA." ATKINS LOOKED OUT THE rider's window of the police cruiser. "Did you see that?"

"What, what?" Sergeant Hanson braked the cruiser. "What is it?"

"An unbelievable meteor, didn't you see it?"

"No, I'm driving."

"It was really bright and really close. I swear it must've hit just a couple of miles over there to the east, or less. In the direction of Shady Acres."

"Convenient."

"Yeah. Convenient."

When the two policemen pulled up to Dora Pearcy's trailer a few minutes later, there was no light on inside.

"Mrs. Pearcy." Hanson knocked several times on the door of the old woman's trailer. "Mrs. Pearcy, it's the police. Open up, please."

"Maybe she's not home," Atkins said.

"Where in the world would she go?"

"I don't know."

"Mrs. Pearcy." Hanson repeated several more times.

"Let's go." Atkins fidgeted around.

"Shh," Hanson hissed. "Listen."

The policemen heard some shuffling from inside the trailer, some low mumbling, and then a light came on.

"Thank God you're here, oh, thank God." Dora Pearcy suddenly threw open her narrow front door. "They were coming in."

"Who was coming in?" Hanson reflexively reached down for his handgun, a 9mm Glock.

He peered past Mrs. Pearcy but could see no one else in the trailer. Atkins, hand on his weapon as well, checked the rest of the area around and behind them.

"Them." Dora pointed toward the back wall of her trailer and the small window there.

"Keep me covered." Hanson told his partner. "And watch for movement out here."

"Affirmative."

"Come on in." Hanson called from the doorway just a few moments later. "False alarm."

"False alarm?" Atkins stepped up into the trailer. Despite the all clear, he kept one hand near his pistol. "What's up?"

"Would you like to tell Atkins what you told me, Mrs. Pearcy?" Hanson rolled his eyes for the benefit of his partner.

"They were coming in after me," Dora said. "Spacemen. Just like on the covers of those magazines at the grocery store. I saw them, I swear. They were right there in the window, just as plain as the nose on your face. They want me. They want to give me tests." The police officers exchanged knowing glances.

"What kind of tests, ma'am?" Atkins repressed a smile.

"I don't want to talk about it." Dora didn't look at either policeman.

"Oh, no?" Hanson picked up the thread. "Why not?"

"Because they're bad, and they give bad tests. They check you in places they shouldn't. It hurts."

"Can you describe these, uh, spacemen to us, Mrs. Pearcy?" Hanson inquired politely.

"Everyone's seen them." Dora told the officers. "They're on the cover of those magazines like I told you."

"Tall? Skinny? Fat?" Hanson winked at Atkins.

"You don't believe me," Dora said. "You think I made this up. Well, they're out there, I tell you. They're just waiting."

"Waiting for what, Mrs. Pearcy?" Hanson said.

"Waiting to take me to their ship, of course. What did you think?"

"Have they been here before?" Atkins said.

"I told you they give me tests."

"Sorry, ma'am." The corporal apologized.

"When were they here before, Mrs. Pearcy?" Hanson picked up the questioning again.

"Right after my late husband, Everett, my third husband, passed away." Dora reflected. "Yes, that was when they came."

"He died rather sudden like, didn't he?" Hanson said. The old woman looked down at her feet and muttered something. "What was that, ma'am?"

"I said." Dora answered in a little bit of a screech that caught both policemen slightly off guard. "He had a weak stomach."

"That's interesting, Mrs. Pearcy, because Atkins and I were just driving over to see you about another gentleman with a 'weak' stomach."

"What?" Dora grunted. "What's that?"

"Did you make dinner for your neighbor, Mr. Chase, earlier tonight, Mrs. Pearcy?"

"Mr. Chase?" Dora looked confused.

"Your neighbor, Mr. Chase. Earlier tonight. Dinner."

"I don't—I, uh…."

"Mr. Chase apparently ate something that didn't agree with him tonight." Hanson explained. "He had to go to the Emergency Room at the hospital. Had his stomach pumped. The doctors ran some tests to see what might have caused the problem. They won't be ready until the morning, but since Mr. Chase told us he had eaten here with you tonight, we thought we should check and see if you knew what might have caused him to get sick."

"Me?" Dora looked from one policeman to the other. "How would I? Oh… my. But what about the spacemen? What about them?"

"Mrs. Pearcy." Hanson said gently. "We need you to stay here on Planet Earth with us right now. Poor Mr. Chase is sick."

"Poor Mr. Chase." Dora parroted.

"Can you think of anything you made Mr. Chase tonight that might have made him sick, Mrs. Pearcy?" Atkins said.

"Made him?" Dora's eyes glazed over. "Made him."

"Never mind, ma'am," Atkins said. "We'll come back to see you in the morning after the tests are in. We'll have a better idea then."

"A better idea." Dora repeated.

"Ma'am," Hanson said, "please try to understand this. Do not go anywhere tonight, all right? Stay here. We'll be back early in the morning to see you. Okay?"

"You have to go?" Dora wondered. "Now? What about them?"

"Them?" Atkins said.

"The spacemen." Hanson told his partner.

"Oh." Atkins snapped his fingers.

"Please don't go." Mrs. Pearcy suddenly begged the officers. "Please. They're waiting out there for me. They're going to take me away. And give me bad tests. Probes. Probes they call them."

"We have to go now, ma'am," Hanson said, "but we'll do a thorough check around the trailer before we leave. You'll be all right. You'll be fine."

"Please." Dora weakly moaned as the policemen made their way back outside. "Please." She stood in the doorway while the officers made their check of the area around the trailer.

"It's okay, Mrs. Pearcy." Hanson called back from beside the police car. "No one is in sight. Everything is okay. We'll see you in the morning."

"In the morning." Dora swayed back and forth in the doorway as the policemen drove off into the night. "In the morning... morning."

———

THE POLICE OFFICERS HAD BEEN gone less than five minutes when the others came for Dora. She made no effort to resist them. All resistance was, as she had heard someone say, futile. They came out of her closets, from under the trailer, from the stand of trees just beyond Shady Acres. There were so many of them.

"Are you ready to go, Mrs. Pearcy?" their leader said. His big black eyes were dull and expressionless.

"Where?" Dora already knew the answer and dreaded what would go on when they got to their destination. "Where are we going?"

"To a better place," the lead one said, although Dora doubted his truthfulness. "To a far better place."

"Oh, my." Dora patted the curlers on her head. "Oh my, indeed."

———

THE FIRST THING SERGEANT HANSON and Corporal Atkins did the morning after they had visited Dora Pearcy at her trailer in the Shady Acres Trailer Park was stop by the hospital for the test results on what had made old Mr. Chase so sick. With a photocopy of those results placed between them in the police cruiser they drove straight back to Mrs. Pearcy's mobile home. The lights were on in the trailer, but the front door was wide open, and it didn't look as if anyone was inside

"Lights are on, but it don't look like anybody's home." Atkins joked as the policemen parked their vehicle in front of Dora's trailer.

"You check around the outside of the trailer." Sgt Hanson did not laugh. "I'll go inside."

"Got it." Atkins wiped the smile off his face. "But holler if you see anything. I got your back."

"Right. I'll be careful."

Atkins, hand resting on his pistol, walked cautiously around the trailer looking for what he wasn't sure. All he saw were some flattened down places in the sparse grass and something that looked like strips of gelatin that had been dropped at odd intervals behind the home. He was bent down more closely inspecting the gelatinous material when Hanson called to him.

"Coming." Atkins scurried around the side of the trailer to the front door. "What's up?"

"Nothing."

"Nothing? What do you mean?"

"Just that. There's no sign of the old lady. None at all."

"You checked inside?"

"Yeah."

"Everywhere?"

"I said I checked."

"You suppose she knew we were coming back?"

"Let's check everything again," Hanson said.

The policemen checked Dora Pearcy's trailer again from front to back, side to side, each cabinet, closet, room—every inch of the place. All they found were some burnt places around two windows, windows that were partially pushed open.

"I got a funny feeling about this." Hanson commented as the officers stood again in the doorway of the trailer.

"She must've known we finally had the goods on her," Atkins said. "Still, she couldn't have got far."

"I don't know."

"Don't know? What? You're not buying into that spacemen thing she was jabberin' on about, are you? Come on."

"Well, she's certainly not here."

"Let's take the cruiser and drive around," Atkins said. "We'll find her. She's probably only a few blocks from here."

"Yeah, maybe so. She's bound to be close by."

But the policemen, after driving all over town and half the county, could find no trace of Dora Pearcy. She was nowhere to be found. There was no sign of her whatsoever.

After a few days, she officially became a missing person. The lecherous Mr. Chase, his stomach pumped clean, made a full recovery, vowing never to pursue older women again. In time, Sergeant Hanson and Corporal Atkins made fewer and fewer trips to Dora's trailer in Shady Acres until the case became cool, cooler, cold.

It was, the policemen had to admit to themselves if not to others, as if Dora Pearcy had disappeared into thin air. She never returned to her trailer in Shady Acres nor to anywhere in the area, as far as anyone ever knew. It seemed that she had, indeed, left this world, that she had vanished from the very face of the earth.

———————————

DORA WOKE TO BLACKNESS AND a mild headache. After a moment, she could see the light from a small porthole off to the left. In the distance, far below and behind her it seemed, she could hear the faint pounding of some kind of machine, perhaps a large engine.

Blinking, she rolled slightly onto her side and peered out the little porthole nearby. The deep black sky beyond was punctuated by myriad, crisply bright stars or other heavenly bodies. Heavenly bodies that were moving, or being moved past, at a rapid rate.

"Oh," she whispered, fearful of her new surroundings. "My goodness."

A brushing sound close by caused her to stop speaking immediately. She could tell she was not alone. She could feel the presence of others there with her, there in the dark. Suppressing an instinct to cry out, she squeezed her own body within itself, trying to become as small and inconspicuous as possible. Suddenly, she felt them all move around her, brushing against her, touching her with their long, angled limbs.

"Relax, Mrs. Pearcy." A nearby voice caused her to involuntarily jerk her body upwards, off the metal, bunk-like surface upon which she lay. The voice sounded like someone speaking from the bottom of a well lined with steel. "Take a deep breath. Everything is going to be all right."

"No, no." She cried out plaintively, uselessly, as innumerable scrawny arms and bony fingers began touching her, nudging her, probing her—in places that weren't proper. "Please."

"It will all be over soon. Just lie back and relax. This won't hurt a bit."

"Aaagh!" She groaned, surrendering to the unspeakable acts being perpetrated upon her by these heinous beings.

Taking in a huge lung full of air, she released it with a mighty scream that commingled equal parts terror and pain. But it was no use. Who was there to hear her cries, who there to save her, who indeed? No one. Not now. Not ever.

They had finally come for her—just as she had known they would and there was no remedy for it. She would never see her home again, or go to Bingo, or see her little patch of the trailer park with that filthy old Mr. Chase.

"We're going to take your curlers off now." The tinny, echo-like voice was close to her ear.

"What?" She fretted, thinking of her messy, thinning hair being seen by so many strange beings all at one time. "What?"

"You won't be needing them anymore."

"No. No, of course not."

"Just lie back now, and let us finish our job."

"Yes." She finally acquiesced as a warm, golden sensation flowed over and through her tired old body.

The worst wasn't so bad when it finally happened to you, she remembered having heard someone say once in a movie or something. She was beyond it all, now, anyway. She had been taken up, beyond her little trailer park, beyond the petty worries and concerns of her day to day life, beyond the blue-green orb of the earth itself.

"Yes," she said, as the probes moved in and out and over her body from every conceivable angle. "Yes."

Dora was content finally, even happy. The probes no longer hurt. She breathed deeply and closed her eyes. She was at peace, fully relaxed. A little smile played along the edges of her dry lips. She could see long, angled limbs and fingers waving akimbo above her, around her, hurrying to their tasks. But the little smile on her lips did not fade. It remained as it was, unchanging, unaltered, eternal.

TIERRA Y LIBERTAD

"LISTEN, SIR." DETECTIVE SERGEANT JESUS "Chuy" Guajardo addressed his superior officer, Lieutenant Vicente Carranza. "You've got to let me talk to Emiliano before we bring him down. He's been on the force too long to deserve less than a chance to explain himself."

"And," Carranza said, "he's been your friend for even longer than that."

"Our friendship has nothing to do with the case."

"Come on, anybody else you would've brought down long ago. We brought you into Internal Affairs, Guajardo, because of your unquestioned reputation. You may be the cleanest cop the department has ever had."

Chuy lowered his head.

"But, your friendship with this proven dirty cop is clouding your judgment, and it's making you and us look bad. There can be no hint, not a whisper, of favoritism or anything else negative regarding IA. You know that."

"Yes, sir, but this is different."

"How?"

"Just let me talk to him. Emiliano will listen to me."

"We know you go back to academy days together, but your friend has been throwing his weight around with the locals, running thugs in the neighborhoods. He may have been a great cop once, but now he's got to be reined in."

"If I can just see him, talk to him, Lieutenant."

"You have one chance." Carranza brusquely turned his back on Chuy. "We shipped him down to El Centro on a temporary assignment. Go see him. Convince him to come in on his own. And don't let him take you with him if he won't. You're walking on thin ice as it is."

"Yes, sir, I'll drive down today."

"Get to it, then." Carranza ended the conversation with a dismissive wave of his hand. "Go."

THE HEAT INCREASED EXPONENTIALLY AS Chuy drove down out of the mountains away from San Diego and into the western edges of the Imperial Valley. He turned on the air conditioning but found himself sweating anyway. He was not looking forward to confronting his long-time friend Emiliano Zaragoza. They had been through a lot together. Gangs, drug busts, murder investigations.

They had weathered many a storm, fought side by side to uphold the law. But slowly Emiliano had changed, began to disappear for long stretches of time during their assigned shifts, was rumored to be associating with "connected" dealers, shakers, and other unsavory characters. Chuy had warned his partner but to no avail. Now Emiliano had been exiled to El Centro, and he had to convince his friend to give himself up voluntarily or be arrested. It was as clear cut as that.

Wiping beads of perspiration off his forehead, he noticed that the outside heat was overpowering the air conditioning inside the car. It got hotter and hotter, and he sweated more and more. The sun beating down caused the highway before him to waver and wobble, so much so that it looked as if water were floating over the road.

Blinking in the bright light, he drove on, watching the watery apparition on the highway dance and bob, always fading as the car neared, always reappearing further up ahead. He tried not to focus on the unfolding mirage before him.

As he neared the community of Plaster City, an unexpected collection of industrial buildings in the middle of nowhere north of the highway, he began to feel something more than the heat, something odd. The heat waves on the road began to dance vertically now, like a wet curtain swaying back and forth, up and down, mesmerizing, tantalizing, strange.

Unlike the earlier mirages, this wavering curtain seemed to be coming toward him rather than receding as his vehicle sped toward it. It was getting closer and closer. He eased up on the gas, but there was no way to stop in time. Instinctively ducking his head, he drove right through the curtain.

"*Dios mío!*" He cried out. "My God!"

HEAT WAVES SHIMMERED AND FLOATED, dancing like a phantom stream hovering over the trail, tiny sparkles of light glistening from crushed rock in the roadbed. For several moments, he struggled to find his bearings, to clear his mind. On either side of him were heavily-armed men wearing large Mexican sombreros. They were on horseback. How odd, he thought, only to realize that he, too, was astride a powerful horse thundering down the trail.

"*Que es esto?*" He cried out. "What is this?"

Yet, he rode easily, comfortably, in the small *vaquero's* saddle tied firmly to the back of the snorting, puffing horse. Ahead, he saw a small, white-washed, stucco house—more of a hut—some fifty yards off to the right of the trail.

"*Aquí, Jefe.*" A rider beside him called out. *Jefe?* Boss of what?

Slowing the pace of their horses, he and the other riders—there were four others with him—left the trail, heading toward the little house.

"This is it, *Jefe.*" The rider beside him said, as if "it" had some clear meaning that only Chuy was not aware of.

"It? It what?"

"This is the place of the traitor to Emiliano." The other man raised an eyebrow. "You are having second thoughts?"

"Uh—Emiliano sent us to do this?"

"*Sí.* He told me, 'Luis, take Jesus and some men and eliminate the traitor Gonzalez. He is an agent of Carranza. The worst kind of man. A dog. Have Jesus do the job.'"

"Me? Why me?"

"You are the newest. It is a test. You must prove your loyalty to Emiliano by killing the traitor. You are up to it, no?"

"Kill him?"

"*Como no?* Of course."

"I don't know this man I must kill."

"He is a traitor to Emiliano, that is all you need to know."

"I...."

Luis raised that eyebrow again.

"It is the only way to show that you yourself are not an agent of Carranza. That you are not here to assassinate Emiliano yourself."

"Why would I do that?"

"It is your choice. You kill the traitor Gonzalez and win the *Gran* Emiliano's trust or we shoot you."

Chuy looked around at the other riders. They all looked the same, from their big sun-blocking sombreros to their tightly-pointed cowboy boots. They wore loose peasant shirts, tight pants with stripes down the sides, and to a man were heavily armed. They all seemed to have the same sardonic smile that the one called Luis displayed.

Chuy fully understood the mission now. Kill or be killed. Inside he felt a powerful rage for Emiliano but instinctively knew to keep it to himself. Now was not the time to reveal himself. Now it was necessary to stay calm and force his anger deep down inside.

"Where is the traitor Gonzalez?"

There was an audible release of breath by the mounted men beside him.

"Paco, Roberto." Luis called over to two of the men. "Get the *cabrón* out of his rat hole."

"*Sí,* Luis." Paco and Roberto answered like the good soldiers they were.

They dismounted quickly and, with pistols drawn, carefully entered the little house. Those remaining outside heard scuffling, shouting, but no weapons were fired. In just moments more, a man was suddenly shoved through the doorway and out into the bright light. Behind him came Paco with his pistol at the man's back. Roberto followed, pushing a young woman forward. The woman spat on the ground when she saw Luis and Chuy.

"Very stylish." Luis said.

"Go to the devil," the woman snarled. "Pig."

Roberto grabbed the woman by the hair causing her to cry out.

"Let the woman be." Chuy ordered.

"*Bien.*" Roberto released the woman's hair. "Okay."

The woman pulled away from Roberto but still scowled fiercely at Chuy and Luis.

"Fire. Lots of fire." Luis said to Roberto. "Get her out of here. But do not harm her."

"*Sí.*" Roberto pulled the struggling woman out of harm's way.

"You, Gonzalez," Luis said, when it was just the men. "Your time has finally come."

"To hell with you." Gonzalez said.

"We'll see you there." Luis looked over at Chuy who pulled his pistol out of its holster.

"*Cobardes.*" Gonzalez spit. "Cowards."

Chuy aimed his pistol at the condemned man. Gonzalez looked him straight in the eye. Chuy saw the recognition there, remembered that they had met in Mexico City, knew the man, knew who he was.

"You," Gonzalez said.

"*Tierra y Libertad.*" Chuy yelled. "Land and Freedom."

"*Tierra y Libertad.*" The other men echoed the cry of the Zapatista movement loudly.

"I know y—" Gonzalez began.

Chuy shot him three times. The man's final words died on his lips.

On the short ride back to the *Gran* Emiliano's *hacienda*, Chuy fretted about the close call with Gonzalez. He knew the man had recognized him, was getting ready to identify him as a traitor to Emiliano. Sweat soaked his clothes as they rode, and it was not all from the heat of the day.

In Gonzalez, he had killed one from his own side—just to prove to Luis and the others that he could be trusted around Emiliano and was not an infiltrator, not a snitch, not a traitorous spy. But he was those things, and he sweated more, and hated. Hated Emiliano, hated the circumstances that forced him to choose between the way of his superiors, the rule of supposed law, and that of a man he had grown to respect and admire.

Still, it was his job, and he had taken it on willingly. He also knew this job could be his last, ever. He might not survive doing what he had to do. It had to be done fast and with finality. He steeled himself for the challenge.

"*Oyé,*" Luis cried out as the group rumbled into Emiliano's *hacienda* grounds. They rode straight up to the main house with its fancy balcony where the *Gran Jefe* awaited them. "It is done."

Luis waved his pistol around. A couple of the *vaqueros* shot rounds into the air.

Good. Make it loud. The sound would protect him.

Emiliano, smiling, took the stairs down into the center grounds to greet his victorious soldiers who dismounted, all save Chuy, to receive the thanks of their boss.

"*Bueno, vaqueros,*" Emiliano patted his men on the shoulders, "well done, well done." He looked up at Chuy, who remained astride his horse. "And did our new man pass his test?"

"*Si, Jefe,*" Luis said. "He shot the traitor dead."

"That's what it was to you, nothing but a test?" Anger rose in Chuy to match his hatred. "I killed to show you I would?"

"*Como no?*" Emiliano replied. "How else am I to know? You could be sent from Carranza. It happens."

"You are so important that innocent men must die to prove another's loyalty?" Chuy moved a hand slowly toward his pistol.

"What is this?" Emiliano cocked his head to one side.

Chuy knew it was time. It was now or never. He had shown too much of his hand. He had fooled Emiliano up to now, but the cloud of friendship and loyalty he had built over the past months was rapidly falling from the *Gran Jefe's* eyes. Emiliano began to reach for his own weapon. Chuy got to his first.

"Die, cabrón." He fired three fast rounds directly into Emiliano's chest at short range. "Death to you and death to *Tierra y Libertad.*"

Emiliano's men rushed to their *jefe's* side, and in that instant of concern for their fallen leader, Chuy spurred his horse, rode hard toward the gates of the hacienda and the freedom of the countryside. He heard yelling behind him, he heard pistols fired, he heard the air whistle with the sound of metal rounds seeking his body. He rode on hard, fast, faster—on into the blazing land.

The hot sun bore down on man and rider as they charged across the earth seeking escape. He drove the animal hard, pushed it to its limits. He could hear the men behind them now on horseback, pursuing, gaining. Dirt kicked up around him from their shots. They were getting closer by the minute.

Ahead, he saw a heavy, wavering heat mirage dancing, rising from the burning soil. He rode his horse hard for that wave, headed him straight for it. Behind, he heard the cries of Emiliano's *vaqueros,* heard them curse his name, heard the staccato report of their pistols. Galloping through the curtain of heat, Chuy and horse bolted over a small sand hill, down onto a flat plain, away from their pursuers, away from the treachery and death of the *Gran* Emiliano.

CHUY SHOOK HIS HEAD AS if it had become entangled in some unseen cobweb. The concrete ribbon of highway approaching El Centro stretched out before him. He unintentionally slowed his vehicle, releasing pressure on the gas pedal without fully realizing it.

Seeing a wide space by the side of the road he guided the car out of traffic. He stopped a few feet off the pavement and rested for a moment. What in the world had just happened? Had he had a vision? Had he somehow gone somewhere, to some other place, some other time?

One thing was for sure. He was overwhelmed by a sense of guilt and shame. How could he be such a coward, such a turncoat? How could he betray a friend like Emiliano? Even when he knew that friend had done wrong, had perhaps become bad.

It was all a relative thing. Wrong or bad to whom? What was more important—friendship, trust, your own self-respect, or the absolute letter of the law—the law that he had sworn to uphold?

Well, he thought, I have come this far. I have been sent to do a job. I must see it through. I have to find out from Emiliano himself, and then I will make my decision. Then I will choose. Slowly pulling back out onto the highway, he headed for El Centro and the last known location he had for Emiliano.

THE *GATO NEGRO* BAR AND Billiards Hall was a block west of Imperial Avenue, the first exit in El Centro and the road that would tie up with Highway 86 running north to Imperial and Brawley. Chuy parked his car on the street just down from the *Gato Negro* and put his police pistol under the driver's seat. If he didn't carry it with him, he couldn't use it.

Coming in out of the bright sunlit day, the bar was totally dark. He paused inside the door for a moment before walking on into the club. He heard some men talking and the cracking sound of pool balls being hit. Just as he was regaining his vision, a man appeared directly in front him.

"May I help you, *señor?*"

Chuy could make out that the man was short, stocky and, from the tone of his voice, a person who was used to being listened to.

"I'm looking for a friend of mine." He explained, now able to see the man better. He was indeed a thick man, with a bulge under one shoulder that was not muscle-related. A couple of other men in the place were also taking note of Chuy's presence.

"Aren't we all," the man said, without humor.

"Emiliano," Chuy said. "I'm looking for Emiliano."

"Yes?"

"Tell him it is Chuy, his partner."

"Un momento."

The man started to walk toward the bar when a familiar voice stopped him in his tracks.

"It's okay, Hector." Emiliano called out from back by the pool tables. "No problem. We are friends."

"Muy bien, Jefe." Hector turned back to face Chuy. "You don't mind?" Chuy offered no resistance to the careful frisking. "He's clean, Boss."

"Thank you, Hector." Emiliano came up to the two men.

As the two police partners greeted each other, Hector stood to one side, a hand not far from the bulge in his coat.

"I knew you would come for me." Emiliano told Chuy after the old friends had shaken hands.

"Me or someone else."

"You believe the things they say about me, then?"

"I make no judgement."

"And yet you are here."

"I had to be here."

"To see if it was true?"

"Yes."

"Well?"

"Is it true?"

"What would you do if it was?"

"Before today," Chuy said, "I would have arrested you, taken you back. Now...."

"Now?"

"Now, I haven't yet made up my mind."

"If I told you that everything bad you heard about me was true," Emiliano said, "that I had done all the bad things they say. What then? What would you do? Are you here to take me back?"

"I'm here because it was my job. I was sent here to clean up the situation."

"Did they send you to kill me?"

"He don't have a gun, Boss." Hector interjected.

"He wouldn't need one," Emiliano said. Hector moved his hand closer to the bulge in his jacket. Emiliano waved him off. "What'll it be?" He again spoke to Chuy. "Make a choice. It's now or never. You decide. You choose."

Chuy took a deep breath. He thought about his friend's predicament, his own. He remembered the vision of his betrayal in the odd experience he had on the road coming down from San Diego. The choice he faced was too hard now, too hard. He couldn't live with being the kind of man who turned on a close friend, one who put duty above fraternity. Not anymore. Someone else would have to bust Emiliano. Someone else would have to bring him to justice. It would not be him, not Jesus Guajardo.

And he understood the choice he was making. He understood its consequences, how it would be seen by his superiors, his fellow officers. But there was nothing to be done about it. He was not the same man he'd been when he left San Diego. He could no longer live by the book—and he knew what that would mean for him and his career.

Without another word, he turned and walked out of the bar. Outside, it was still hot, and he felt the sweat begin to pop out on his back. Climbing into his car, he buckled up, pulled his shirt away from his body, and cranked the engine. Behind him, Emiliano and Hector stood just outside the door of the *Gato Negro* watching. Hector had one hand near that bulge in his jacket.

Chuy saw them in his peripheral vision as he drove down the street back to Imperial Avenue but did not look at them directly. When he turned right to return to the interstate, he glanced over, but the men were no longer in front of the bar. Releasing a deep breath, he drove on, on through town and out to I-8.

Turning right onto the San Diego exit, he tried to let the emotions of this strange and critical day in his life drain from his body like the sweat produced by the Imperial Valley heat. Turning up his air conditioner, he drove back toward San Diego, on toward an uncertain future.

About the time he reached Plaster City, he reached into his shirt pocket and pulled out his detective's badge. He looked it over for a moment, considered it carefully and then tossed it casually onto the rider's seat beside him. It rode there all the way back to San Diego. He never picked it up again.

COYOACAN

DRIVING ACROSS TOWN, JACK MERCADER could feel a headache coming on. Just thinking of old Lev Bronstein and his officious, annoying old wife was enough to practically cause a migraine. Lev was ill-tempered and demanding, his wife distant and mistrustful while being intolerably solicitous of her husband.

Pulling up to a stop sign in the couple's neighborhood, with the expected white picket fences, well-mowed lawns, and clean streets, he removed his glasses and massaged the bridge of his nose with the thumb and forefinger of his right hand. He was definitely getting a headache.

He had been working for the Bronsteins a little over a month. Two nights a week he went to their home to ostensibly help type and edit a book of essays that Lev, a former college political science teacher, had been working on for the better part of a decade. In reality, all Jack did was see to the steady stream of trivial demands issued by the old man.

"Get me a cup of coffee." Lev ordered gruffly. "A pen. A pad. An eraser. This. That. Get me, get me, get me."

In the short time he'd been coming to the Bronstein's, Jack had learned to totally mistrust the Mrs. who, after frowning at him when he first arrived, would then scurry to the back of the house and lurk behind doors, listening to Jack and Lev's conversation, waiting, he was sure, for him to make any kind of mistake.

No wonder his head ached. No wonder he had of late been harboring socially unacceptable ideas in his head about eliminating Lev and his constant barrage of demands and complaints. His last visit had been the worst yet.

"My husband is a great man." Mrs. Bronstein corralled him in the doorway before he even had a chance to get back to Lev's study.

"Yes, ma'am." His tone was not as deferential as it should have been.

The old woman huffed off to a back room near the study complaining about the quality of help available these days. He forced himself to the task of being Mr. Bronstein's typist, gopher, and assistant flunky.

"You're late," Lev said.

"Sorry, sir."

"Get me some paper then will you? If you're here to get some work done."

"Yes, sir," Jack replied meekly, thinking how he'd like to tell the old man where to go. At least once.

Lev kept up his badgering for nearly the entire three hours Jack worked. He ordered him to bring tea, to retype several pages that he insisted Jack had failed to key enter correctly, and to painstakingly transcribe several minutes of notes that he, Lev, had recorded the night before.

Jack could feel an outburst of anger coming on and had left the room over Lev's objections. The Mrs. darted in to her husband's side, and Jack could hear them bitterly complaining about his poor work habits and lack of professionalism.

At that moment, he spotted a small, but sharp-pointed axe, the kind rock hunters use, lying on a shelf out in the hallway away from Lev's study. He picked up the axe, turned it over in his hands, felt its weight and balance, considered how effective its use might be on the skull of a whining, sexagenarian. While these murderous thoughts ran through his mind, Lev howled for him to get back into the study and do his duty.

"Coming, sir." Jack made a mental note to put the axe where he could slip it under his coat when he left that night.

Now, as he pulled up to the curb fronting the Bronstein's home and parked his car, head throbbing, he felt the inside of his coat pocket for the small axe. Could he actually do something so vile? Could he actually kill another person? His mind told him no, but his aching head said yes. Without Lev and his constant harassing, the pain would go away. His mind would become clear, he would be free.

Sighing deeply, he laid his arms across the steering wheel and nestled his head, face down, into the comfortable, vertical lap he had created. As he rested there momentarily, he noticed an abrupt, brief change in the lighting around him. Perhaps a large cloud had just passed overhead, temporarily blocking out the sun.

Whatever it was, he enjoyed the diminished sunlight. The reduction in brightness seemed to help his headache. For a minute or so, he remained in his face-down position, resting, gathering himself. At last, and coincident with the return of the outside light, he raised his head. He could tell immediately that something odd had occurred. Things were just not quite right.

Climbing gingerly out of his car and walking around to the sidewalk, he felt slightly disoriented. For one thing, the Bronsteins's house was set back further from the street than he remembered. The surrounding area, rather than being full of aging middle-income houses, was more upscale, grander, with lusher vegetation.

The place had a semi-tropical look and feel to it. He noticed a street sign not far away and marveled at the names thereon—Viena and Río Churubusco. How peculiar. Nearby was a sign advertising Plaza Hidalgo, Coyoacan. None of this was making sense. And when he looked back at the Bronsteins's house, not only was it definitely set farther back from the road than he remembered, but there were two uniformed men coming down the sidewalk leading up to the house. Guards? He didn't remember any such thing from before.

"What's your business?" One of the guards blocked his way up the sidewalk. Even though he was sure the guard had not spoken in English, Jack somehow understood perfectly.

"I—I'm here to help, Lev, uh, Mr. Bronstein."

"He means *Señor* León," the other guard explained.

"Oh, yes," the first guard said. "Now I remember. You are the assistant. You help the *señor* writer."

"That's right." Jack again stuttered.

He was a little confused by the presence of the guards, especially when he felt the small pick axe hidden in the pocket of his coat bump against his side.

"This is *Señor* Mornard." The second guard waved a hand to indicate recognition of the new arrival.

"Jacques Mornard?" The first guard checked a sheet of paper on a small clipboard.

"*Sí,*" the second guard confirmed. "This is he."

"Now I remember you," the first guard said. "From the other day. You can go in now."

"Thank you." Jack wondered why Jacques Mornard sounded like it actually was his name. In some unexplained way, it seemed right.

By the time he reached the front door, things had become much more familiar. There was Mrs. Bronstein, as usual, greeting him with her beady, suspicious eyes.

"Why are you here again today?"

"Who is it, Mama?" Lev's voice could be heard from inside the house.

"It's that boy, Jacques," the Mrs. screeched. "Mornard. I don't know why he's here."

"Your husband and I have unfinished business." Jack acquiesced not only to the new name but to the new situation in which he found himself, as well.

The old woman grunted, but she opened the door and let Jacques inside the house.

He wasn't the only one who hated Lev Bronstein. He walked into the main living room. Across the back wall of the room, in a semicircle covering several feet, were several bullet holes, a stark reminder of an apparent attempt on Lev's life from sometime before.

He would be doing himself and the world a favor. Lev Bronstein has outlived his usefulness. He may have been great once, but now he is unnecessary, a problem. More powerful and farsighted people than he wanted Lev, or León, out of the picture. Jacques would be the instrument of their wishes.

"Jacques." The old man's voice knocked the erstwhile assistant out of his reverie. "Are you coming or not?"

"I'm coming," he answered, at first gruffly, then milder as he saw the Mrs. poke her head out of a nearby room.

She was ubiquitous, the old hag. She appeared any time Lev called for anything. Always checking to see if the assistant responded properly, efficiently, and quickly.

"Coming, sir."

The old woman vanished into the interior of the house. He made a face in the direction of her disappearance.

"Good morning, *Señor* León." He used the semi-formal tone of the guards to address the great thinker.

"Get the Dictaphone." Lev ordered. "I've got many things to say today. Go on, hurry."

"But, sir. I thought today we would go over the article I wrote for the Party. You said…."

"I said. I said." Lev waved off the suggestion. "There are bigger fish to fry. Bring that machine to me and hook everything up."

"But, sir…."

"But nothing. Work. Work. That's your job here. I'll see to your article another time."

Jacques ground his teeth, felt like slapping the old man, felt the small axe inside his coat. He should do it now, rid the world of this pestilence right this moment. But he did not act. Not yet. He found the Dictaphone machine, hooked it up, and placed the large microphone where Lev could easily speak into it. Went about organizing the typing he'd done the day before. He didn't understand why Lev would speak into the machine today, when he was there to type up whatever ramblings came out of his ancient philosopher's head.

Luckily, Lev only spoke into the machine for about fifteen minutes. That wouldn't be so much work to catch up on, for a change. Seeing the old man set aside the microphone, Jacques decided to re-introduce the article he had written. It was just something he'd dashed off, but now it occurred to him that it might be the catalyst he needed to take care of Lev once and for all. The guards were outside the house, the Mrs. was hiding somewhere. If he got Lev to concentrate on the article, it might be his chance. There would only be one. He was sure of that.

"Well, all right." Lev agreed, however reluctantly, to look over the article.

"Thank you, sir." Jacques replied obsequiously, cringing like a feeble peasant or corrupt courtier before a king.

Just Lev's tone was able to send flames into his mind and blood today. This was definitely going to be the right time. He stood quietly behind the old man, fingering the axe inside his coat.

"No, no." Lev said to himself, no doubt finding flaws in the political logic of the article. "This will never do. Needs more detail."

"You don't like it, sir?" Jacques hovered directly behind the old man, carefully bringing the axe out from beneath his coat. "Something wrong?"

"Rewrite this part here. And this there. Needs a stronger hand."

"A stronger hand, sir?"

Jacques felt the disconnect between himself and the great thinker. He no longer saw him as a person but a thing. He felt himself go cold all over, in his veins, in his heart. He raised the axe and without hesitation brought it down on the top of Lev's head with all his might.

He felt the axe break through the skull bone, felt its edge dig into the old man's brain. And at that moment he heard a cry rise up, a cry deep and elemental, energy-draining, death-signifying. He heard the cry as if it came from far away, either far away without or far away within. He could not tell. He no longer felt linked to the real world. All that remained was the cry. A long sorrowful cry, full of pain, laced with the agony of unfinished life. It was a cry he would never forget, never get out of his head again.

And then Mrs. Bronstein was on him and the guards, as well. The men beat him, slapping and striking him in the face. They pulled him away from Lev, who had stood, holding the top of his head in his hands, then reeled toward the doorway. He watched him stagger away until the barrage of punches from the guards brought the relief of silent, black unconsciousness.

When Jack woke it was with a start, eyes wide open. With a little cry, he lifted his head and pulled himself away from the steering wheel. How long had he been out? What had happened? He reached up timorously, carefully feeling his face, his head. No bruises, no cuts. Nothing. He had a slight headache, but that was all, except....

Except in his head he could still hear the sound of Lev's death cry. He shuddered. Had he really killed Mr. Bronstein? What had occurred, where was he? He remained motionless for several moments, allowing the sound in his head to diminish, to almost fade away.

With considerable trepidation, he focused on the world outside his vehicle. It was a bright and sunny day. And it was the right neighborhood—white picket fences, freshly-mowed lawns. He was in front of the Bronsteins's home. Things seemed normal. He let out a deep sigh that carried with it the last strange sound of Lev's final agony.

"Oh, thank God," Jack said out loud, absorbing again his familiar world, rejoicing in the opportunity it offered, the opportunity still to choose a different path, to make the good, the right choice.

Buoyed by a mild euphoria, he hopped out of his car and headed up the sidewalk to the Bronstein's house. Mrs. Bronstein was waiting for him at the door, her usual suspicious self.

"Good morning, Mrs. B. Nice day."

Mrs. B. grunted something unintelligible and gave him what was meant to be a withering look. He slipped past her into the house.

"Who is that, Mother?" Lev's cranky old voice rasped out from back in his study.

"It's me, Mr. Bronstein. I'm here to help you out."

The old philosopher and writer snorted, but when Jack came into the room he was greeted not by a demand but by a curious look. "Get me some paper?"

"Right away, sir."

Jack was still thrilled that whatever experience he had had, or seemed to have had, was not of the here and now. He could still change. He could choose not to harm another person. He could be better than that.

During the rest of the session, he maintained his new attitude, and Lev responded to it in kind. The complaints were fewer, the demands less harsh. The two men might never be friends, but at least they could work together professionally, without open rancor.

At the first opportunity, when Lev was busy writing, Jack stole out to the hallway. Making sure that Mrs. B. was nowhere in sight, he hurriedly replaced the axe on the shelf. He then looked around for something to completely conceal the would-be weapon.

On a higher shelf, above the one on which the ax rested, he found a small collection of old newspaper clippings. They would perfectly hide the instrument. With only a cursory glance at the papers, the headline of one announcing the arrival of an exiled revolutionist to Mexico City, he spread them in front of and on top of the axe.

"Done." He announced quietly to himself. "No more of that."

As he turned away from the shelf and the axe, he heard his employer beckoning him.

"Jack." The old man's tone was neutral, professional. "Can you help me here, please?"

"Yes, sir, Mr. B." Jack hustled toward the great man's study. "Coming. I'll be right there."

GORKI IN NEW YORK

STEAMING TO AMERICA—APRIL 10, 1906

ON THE VOYAGE TO AMERICA I cautioned restraint. We knew little of that wild, strange land and even less of her people. But Alexei Maximovich would have none of it.

"You are too suspicious," he mildly chided me as we walked the promenade deck, Marya Fyodorovna Andreieva between us holding onto Gorki's arm. Marya Fyodorovna was a lovely woman, but an actress, temperamental and volatile. Not well suited for restraining Maxim's flights of fancy and emotion.

"Possibly, but it is a different culture than ours. Perhaps as different as two cultures may be."

"Nonsense," he said. "America, my good Burenin, is the freest land on earth."

"You are generous, Maximovich," Marya said.

Maxim patted her hand gently. "We must be, for we hope that they will be generous to us and to our cause."

Our cause? I thought. Sometimes it seemed that the Bolshevik cause had become the Gorki cause. Gorki's and the other Russian revolutionists'. Marya and I were not cut from the same cloth as Maxim. This was the man who had been a street urchin at nine in Nihzni-Novgorod, a tramp, a worker on the Volga, and then a great writer.

Maxim was a friend of the late Chekhov and of the magnificent Tolstoy. He was a real man of the people, a true radical, a celebrated ex-prisoner of his majesty the czar. He had become Gorki the international sensation.

Marya Fyodorovna was a beautiful woman, marvelous actress, and loyal companion to Maxim—even a fine "aunt" to his little boy and girl. She was accepted, however reluctantly, by Ekaterina Pavlovna, Gorki's estranged but still legally recognized wife.

As for me, I was a competent secretary and translator, nothing more, but Maxim—he was the Gorki—the "bitter" one, one of the most famous men in the world.

"I believe, Maximovich," I said, "that your generosity and your openness can be as harmful to you as useful. I don't trust the reporters nor the Germans we dine with each night, and you know there's even at least one czarist spy here on board with us."

"Ah, Burenin, you have far too low an opinion of yourself and you place it on those around you."

"Nikolai Evgenievich is right about the spy, though, my dear husband," Marya Fyodorovna said.

"Of course, my dear, but what of it? How can a spy hurt me? I've already been a guest of our kind czar. Besides, we are no longer in Mother Russia."

"True enough, Maximovich," I said, "but surely you see the need for circumspect...."

"Hush." Gorki raised his left hand. "Enough. Look there." He pointed into the hazy distance. "Is that not land? Is that not America?"

Suddenly a great cry rose up on the boat, temporarily overwhelming the steady pounding of her steam engines. Passengers rushed to the side of the boat for a first glimpse of the golden promised land. Maxim was beside himself with excitement and joy.

"America! America! America!" He leaned perilously against the railing. Marya held onto him for fear he would fall overboard. "I have been waiting years for this moment. Columbus could not have been more anxious to discover America than I."

For perhaps a quarter of an hour then, Maxim stood with his arms crossed at the railing, his gaze fixed on the slowly approaching shore. Marya and I stood behind and allowed him, as was his wont at great moments, to be alone with his thoughts and emotions.

ARRIVAL—APRIL 10

AS WE NEARED THE HOBOKEN pier, a small cutter came out in a steady rain to greet us and we were surprised to see many old friends on board waving and welcoming us to America.

"Look, Maximovich." I pointed at the cutter. "Isn't that Ivan Narodny?"

"Yes, you're right, Nikolaievich." Gorki squinted to see. "It is. Ivan! Ivan Narodny! And our friend Mandelkern, and Abraham Cahan. And there Wilshire. Hallo, hallo."

"Dearest." Marya Fyodorovna pointed to the group of men on the boat who waved back. "In the midst there, by Ivanovich. It's Zinka."

"Where?" Gorki exclaimed, terribly excited at the prospect of seeing his adopted son Zinovii Alexeivich Peshkov after some three years apart.

"There, Maxim." Marya put her hand by Maxim's face and aimed a long, slender finger at the cutter below.

"Yes, I see him now. Zinka, Zinka, hallo. How are you, son?"

Zinka could not hear his father over the sound of the ship's engines but he waved back and jumped up and down with joy. In a short, happy time we steamed on to the Hoboken pier.

AT THE PIER—APRIL 10

WHEN THE KAISER WILHELM DER Grosse finally docked at the Hoboken pier, her clanging, steaming engines silent at last, we were besieged by friends, reporters, anyone who could find a way on board to see Maxim. All of the people from the cutter who greeted us in the harbor were there —including Zinka, who had a most tender reunion with his adopted, and much taller and bigger, father, the toast of Russian letters.

At first Maxim was overwhelmed by the number of people wishing to see him, and Marya and I acted as a shield. Part of his reason for coming to America was, after all, to improve his health, and to rest and regain his strength. We did not want him to weaken from overwork and stress, to decline and fail like his friend, the incomparable, tragic Chekhov.

To that end, the legal necessity of passing through customs—normally an annoyance—became a respite of sorts for Gorki as he good-naturedly responded to the simple questions that would allow him to enter the United States without restriction.

"No," was his answer to the only question the customs officer really cared about. "I am not an anarchist, I am a socialist. I believe in law and order."

Beyond customs, standing patiently in the rain, waited a throng of Gorki enthusiasts and many curious onlookers. When the crowd spotted Maxim coming down the pier, they went wild and lifted him to their shoulders, cheering and jolting him about. He handled it as best he could but when they also tried to lift Marya Fyodorovna, he broke free and stopped the unruly crowd firmly, though without rancor, from mishandling her.

We returned then to customs long enough for the crowd to settle down and the Hoboken police escorted us to waiting carriages. The crowd again became unruly, however, and tried to unhitch the horses and pull Maxim's carriage themselves up to the Manhattan ferry—but the police restrained them and we continued on without further incident.

———————

THE CLUB A DINNER—APRIL 11

IN THE EVENING IVAN NARODNY sponsored a dinner for Maxim at the Club A on Fifth Avenue where Ivan and several other Russian exiles made their home. Mr. Mark Twain, the celebrated American novelist, self-avowed revolutionist and supporter of the freedom movement in Russia, was the principal speaker. Other notables included William Dean Howells, Peter Finley Dunne, and a goodly portion of the better-known Russians and pro-Russian Americans in the city. Maxim's declared goal of raising a large amount of money for the revolution seemed assured by the warmth and generosity shown him and his cause in this our first day in America.

Earlier in the day, still thrilled by all he saw in the New World, Maxim marveled at the Times Building and gazed happily out at the Hudson River.

"Wonderful, wonderful," he exclaimed when we drove by the Times Building. "I mean to know how it is possible to erect such structures before I leave this country."

And from a window in the Hotel Belleclaire, in a quiet moment after he greeted some one hundred guests who called on him during the day, Gorki looked out over the Hudson and with chest swelling from perhaps longing, or nostalgia, addressed the great river below him.

"What," he said with great emotion, Marya Fyodorovna interpreting in English for those nearby, "is this my native Nihzni-Novgorod, and is this the Volga? Then I am at home, indeed."

Later, Marya basked in the limelight as well. Interrupting Maxim who had assured reporters of the great standing in Russia of the American poet Edgar Allan Poe, she told the journalists she believed Poe would rank higher in America if not for the "women who prevent you from loving him as well as you should."

Turning their attention to the beautiful actress, the reporters asked if she ever performed in her husband's plays.

"Oh, yes, but not for quite some time."

"Believe me, gentlemen," Gorki said, "it is due only to my poor health and my political duties that I have not produced more works for my wife to interpret on stage. She is a brilliant actress of great range and depth."

Marya squeezed Maxim's hand and glanced briefly at me. "At present, I am my husband's wife, nothing else, and I don't wish to be before the public in any other capacity."

Later, at the dinner party, our good fortune continued, except for the unavoidable absence of Mr. Howells, and everyone was in good spirits. A sense of brotherhood and camaraderie informed the proceedings and a manifesto formally inaugurating the American movement to help free Russia, read by Mr. Robert Hunter, was well received.

At the head of the speakers' table, Mr. Twain sat between Ivan Narodny and Maximovich with Zinka to Maxim's right acting as translator. Twain and Gorki seemed to get along famously and when the American addressed the group, he praised both Maxim and his cause.

"It is a great honor for me and for all those who desire freedom for the Russian people to welcome Maxim Gorki and his lovely wife Marya to our shores. Mr. Gorki's reputation as a man of experience and travail is well known to most of you and his status as a true man of the people and as an internationally recognized leader in Russian literature is beyond our poor words to enhance. Suffice it to say that I am proud to share the dais with a man of such impeccable qualities and that his cause is my cause as well."

"I am most emphatically in sympathy with the movement now on foot in Russia to make that country free. I am certain that it will be as successful as it deserves to be. Anybody whose ancestors were in this country when we were trying to free ourselves from oppression must sympathize with those who now are trying to do the same thing in Russia."

When it was Maxim's turn, Zinka doing the honors in English, he also began with an encomium for his fellow writer.

"I am glad to meet Mark Twain. I knew him through his writings almost before I knew any other writer. When I was little more than a boy I dreamed of this meeting, hoped for this day—this evening, and it has been a happy meeting, happy beyond all expectation to me. Mark Twain's fame is so well established all the world over that I could not add anything to it by any words of mine."

With the rapt crowd firmly in his corner, Maximovich then launched into his three-pronged fund raising assault—praise for his benefactors, self-deprecation for his own role, and stirring political rhetoric.

"I come to America expecting to find true and warm sympathizers among the American people for my suffering countrymen, who are fighting so hard and bearing so bravely their martyrdom for freedom. Now is the time for the revolution. Now is the time for the overthrow of Czardom. Now! Now! Now! But we need the sinews of war, the blood we will give ourselves. We need money, money, money. I come to you as a beggar that Russia may be free."

After the dinner we attended a reception at the West Ninety-Third Street home of H. Gaylord Wilshire. It was an open affair and innumerable people came and went, most congratulating Maxim on his successful speech, many promising financial support for our cause. Only the brazen appearance of a czarist agent, who spied on us during the voyage on the Kaiser Wilhelm der Grosse, cast a negative light on the wonderful evening. The spy was confronted by Mr. Wilshire and forced to make a hasty exit. Maxim dismissed the incident with a casual flip of his hand.

A DRIVE IN MANHATTAN—APRIL 12

ON THURSDAY MAXIM RECEIVED GUESTS, debated politics, and entertained offers from several contentious newspapers and magazines that sought his impressions of New York City, America, Russia, and the world in general. Late in the day we managed to escape and took an automobile ride through Manhattan.

Maxim, Marya and I joined Mr. Joseph Mandelkern, a real estate magnate who had recently traveled in Russia, in his large touring car. We went down Fifth Avenue toward Central Park and all the way, with either Marya or myself interpreting, Maxim kept up a steady banter. In Central Park he thrilled at the children feeding squirrels while tiny sparrows fought for leftover crumbs.

"Look there." He pointed to the scene with all the delight and wonder of a child.

"Ah, yes." Mr. Mandelkern said. "Mr. Gorki, you are a great lover of nature and animals as I recall."

"Of course." Maxim's eyes sparkled as he spied little houses built in the park for birds and squirrels. "Even the squirrels and the little gray birds seem to realize that they have the right to—what is it you say in your constitution?"

"Life, liberty, and the pursuit of happiness."

"To life, liberty, and the pursuit of happiness."

After Central Park we stopped at the large monument to the victorious Union General, and President, Ulysses S. Grant.

"Wonderful, wonderful," Gorki said in Russian. He pumped the hand of a surprised policeman who had courteously opened our car door. "Thank you so much, you are kind, quite kind indeed."

We smiled at Maxim's exuberance. The officer lifted his hat and scratched the side of his head.

"This is a wonderful country," Maxim said. "It is surely the Promised Land. I hope I shall live to see the day when things are this way in Russia."

Later, as we drove along Riverside Drive, Mr. Mandelkern pointed out the homes of several rich American capitalists.

"You know, Mr. Gorki." He indicated the home of a man named Charles Schwab. "There is as much money in the aggregate among the wealthy men of this city as in all of Russia."

"I have no doubt," Maxim said, "but I hope no part of it will be subscribed to the national loan the Russian government is trying so hard to raise. I think it would be unworthy of any true American to furnish money for the purchase of guns and bullets with which to murder peaceful, liberty-loving Russians who are only trying to gain their freedom."

"Indeed," Mr. Mandelkern agreed gravely. "Indeed so."

MR. TWAIN AND MR. HOWELLS CALL—APRIL 12

IN THE EVENING AFTER OUR drive in Manhattan, Maxim received the two great American writers Mark Twain and William Dean Howells in our suite at the Hotel Belleclaire. For a good half hour, the three men discussed literature in animated but mutually respectful tones. Maximovich used the opportunity to praise, besides his renowned visitors, the British poet Byron, France's Gustave Flaubert, and Alexandre Dumas, pere.

When the meeting ended, Mr. Twain and Mr. Howells invited Maxim to attend a literary dinner to be held in a fortnight. Gorki was pleased to accept the invitation. I escorted the American gentlemen downstairs and in the lobby we were approached by several newspapermen who had apparently been waiting for just such a chance to waylay the two well-known men of letters.

"Mr. Twain, Mr. Twain," a reporter from the Times called out. "Were you visiting Mr. Gorki? What were you discussing?"

"We were guests of Mr. Gorki," Twain confirmed, a bit overwhelmed by some half dozen reporters crowding around him. Mr. Howells hung back, content to let Mr. Twain field the questions. "And we merely discussed the state of literature in the world. That's all."

"Nothing of the Russian revolution or of Mr. Gorki's mission here in America?" a Herald man said.

"No."

"Do both you and Mr. Howells support Mr. Gorki's position with regard to how the revolution may be carried out," Franklin Giddings of the Independent inquired.

"Well, I, uh…." Mr. Twain began, then called back to Mr. Howells. "Come here, Howells. You look as if you have some information. Be a good fellow. Come back here and tell these gentlemen all about our visit with Mr. Gorki. Be sure, of course, to restrict your comments to such private talk as we had, so as to get it in the papers."

The reporters, excepting Giddings, laughed at Mr. Twain's wit. Mr. Howells reluctantly faced the journalists.

"All that we did," he said in a soft voice, "was invite Mr. Gorki to attend a literary gathering in two weeks. Nothing more."

"That's right," Mr. Twain said. "We are going to offer Gorki the literary hospitality of the country. He is big enough for the honor. It is going to be a dinner with only authors and literary men present. We want to do it in proper style, and will have authors not only from New York, but from Chicago, and we may have some literary geniuses from Indiana, where I believe they breed 'em."

The reporters laughed again at the great American humorist and seemed well satisfied with his words. Mr. Twain corralled the reticent Mr. Howells and the two American literary giants each bowed and then hurried on through the Belleclaire's sumptuous lobby away from the lingering reporters and out into the New York spring evening.

A QUIET DAY OF WORK, SPIES, AND SOCIALIST BROTHERS
APRIL 13

ON FRIDAY, MAXIM AWAKENED FEELING poorly. His incipient consumption had flared up and he blamed it on our heavy social schedule since arriving in America. I was commissioned to reschedule his day with an eye toward rest and perhaps a bit of light literary work later on should he feel better. A reception planned for the evening by the Jewish Bund was canceled and Maxim settled in for a quiet day.

Marya Fyodorovna fussed around, waiting on him hand and foot, and by early afternoon he felt a good deal better. As a result, Maxim allowed a few reporters in for a short interview. They were all agog with the news, hardly a surprise to us, that Maxim was being shadowed by a spy. They told us their papers would be filled with this news in tomorrow's, Saturday's, editions. The reporters wondered if Maxim was aware of the agent.

"Of course, it is a constant and expected part of my life."

"Do you know why, specifically, this man is following you and what he is after?" a reporter from the Times said.

Maxim gave me a helpless look after I translated for him. The question had come up so many times before it had become tiresome.

"Nikolai Evgenevich." He looked at me and gave a small gesture toward the reporters.

"Gentlemen," I said, "Mr. Gorki is tired and wishes me to respond to your questions."

"You are, sir?" one of the reporters queried.

"Nikolai Evgenevich Burenin. Mr. Gorki's private secretary."

"Then tell us, please, why is the spy here in America? What does he want?"

"It is our belief this man is an agent of the czar. The Russian government is trying to prove, which they cannot do, we are here to purchase arms for our revolution—to use against the czar and his terror state."

"You deny that is your purpose here? To get arms for the violent overthrow of the Russian government?"

"Absolutely. If it were, your country would be justified in preventing it and would have the legal right to expel us. But it will never happen because we are not here to engage in such criminal acts. We are here simply to elicit support, in the form of monetary donations, for our cause. Nothing more."

My answer seemed to conclude the spy matter but the reporters wanted more of Maxim.

"Mr. Gorki," the Times man said. "Do you consider yourself to be in exile from Russia?"

"In no sense am I an exile," Maxim said. "But while I am at liberty to return to Russia at any time, I have no doubt that I would be arrested and cast into prison—much like your great union leaders in Idaho today—the moment I set foot on Russian soil."

"Will you not return to your homeland, then?"

"When the right moment has come to return, we will go back and brave the danger. But the time has not yet come."

"You believe, then, the czar absolutely means to imprison you if you go home, Mr. Gorki?"

"As you know, gentlemen," Maximovich said, "I have already been the czar's guest and his next door neighbor, so to speak, when I was enjoying his hospitality in the fortress of St. Peter and St. Paul in our lovely capitol of St. Petersburg."

While the reporters chuckled over Maxim's cavalier attitude about his imprisonment and the danger he faced daily as an enemy of the Russian state, Marya Fyodorovna whispered something into his ear.

"Ah, yes," Maxim said, "gentlemen, my lovely wife has reminded me that I did in fact intend to communicate with my fellow socialists Mr. Haywood and Mr. Moyer who are the prisoners in Idaho I alluded to before. Would you care to hear the telegram I will send momentarily?"

The reporters said they did, but one of them—a *World* writer—first had a question for Marya.

"Mrs. Gorki." The man poised pen on paper. "My readers are fascinated by you and your beauty and would like to know how long you and Mr. Gorki have been married?"

Marya looked at both Maxim and me before answering.

"We've been together about three years."

"I thought it had been much long...."

"Excuse me, gentlemen," I interrupted. "Maximovich—er—Mr. Gorki wishes to share the text of his telegram with you and then needs to rest. Mr. Edwin Markham, the artist, will be calling on us shortly. Shall we, please?"

The reporters agreed, although the *World* man did so reluctantly. Maxim and Marya stood beside me as I read the telegram.

"Mr. Gorki has written his communiqué as follows. To W.D. Haywood and Charles Moyer, County Jail, Caldwell, Idaho. 'Greetings to you, my brother Socialists. Courage! The day of justice and deliverance for the oppressed of all the world is at hand. Ever fraternally yours.' Maxim Gorki."

When I finished reading, Maximovich clapped happily and Marya mouthed her thanks behind a gloved hand. The reporters, perhaps surprised by the telegram, nonetheless respected our wishes and withdrew so that we might prepare for the remainder of the evening.

A FIRESTORM OF INDIGNATION—APRIL 14

SATURDAY MORNING BEGAN PLEASANTLY ENOUGH. Maxim woke feeling stronger, so we breakfasted early at the hotel. Then, joined by Zinka, we went for a leisurely drive in the mild spring air. We cut through Central Park, near our hotel, and Maximovich again marveled at the squirrels coming up to people for food and at the many little houses inhabited by innumerable small, gray birds. At Fifty-Fifth Street we cut through to Broadway and headed back to the hotel. Though we chatted happily, the shrill cry of several boys hawking newspapers from a street corner caught our attention.

"We should get all the papers this morning, papa." Zinka said from the rider's seat up front. "And see what they say of the triumphant mission of the great Gorki—writer, revolutionist, fundraiser nonpareil."

"Zinka," Marya Fyodorovna, who sat between Maxim and me in the backseat, said. "How you carry on. You should really be more respectful of your father."

"Oh, but I am. I meant what I said. I meant no disrespect, father."

"Of course you didn't," Maxim said to the boy. "I know it is just your youthful exuberance. I felt it as much myself when I was your age."

"Thank you, father. You have always been much more kind to me than I deserve."

"Now, now." Gorki patted his adopted son on the arm just as the paperboys reached me in the back seat of the vehicle.

"Hey, mister," One of the little urchins cried out. "Buy *The Times?*"

"No, *The Herald.*" Another broke in.

"*The World, The* World." A third called out, thrusting his newspaper toward me.

"Yes," I said, "and yes, and yes."

"Yes?" The boys could hardly believe their luck.

"Yes."

Suddenly I was inundated with newspapers. The boys shoved a half dozen at me at once. I tried to keep track of the American coins as I paid but was sure the boys, who immediately raced back to their street corners, had most certainly taken advantage of me. Maxim dismissed my concern with a laugh and a wave of a hand.

"Just like me as a boy in Nihzni-Novgorod. I was just the same."

We each took a newspaper—except for Maxim who could not read English—and checked it for stories about him. Suddenly, Marya cried out.

"Monstrous, terrible, how could they? How could they do this to us?"

"What is it, my dear?" Maxim said. Zinka and I looked at each other, then at Marya Fyodorovna. "What is it?" Gorki repeated.

"This horrible, horrible paper."

"Which one?" I worried.

"*The World,*" Marya said. "The filthy *World.* Listen to this headline: "*Gorki Brings Actress Here As 'Mme. Gorki.'*"

"What's wrong with that?" Maxim said.

"They say in the story that I am your mistress," Marya said unhappily. "And that you have abandoned your true wife and your children to the whims of fate back in Russia."

"What trash," Gorki said. "This is libel pure and simple."

"This is exactly what we feared," I said, "what Narodny and others warned us about."

"What are you talking about?" Gorki demanded.

"That America was stricter in her attitudes about marriage and relationships than we are in Russia. We were told it might damage our cause if it was revealed."

"That's a fine thing to say, Nikolai Evgenevich," Marya said.

"Hogwash," Gorki huffed.

"I don't mean it to hurt you, either of you," I said. "But it was a risk we chose to take. Now it has apparently come back to hurt us."

"Possibly it will just blow over?" Zinka suggested.

"We can hope so." I doubted my own hope.

"Let's get back to the hotel," Gorki said emphatically. "We can better judge our position from there, if in fact this filth truly attaches itself to us and is no more than another bump in our long road to success and freedom."

"I suppose," Marya said, "we will find out who are friends are now, won't we?"

"Yes, my dear," Gorki said. "I'm certain that we will."

Back at the Hotel Belleclaire, the reporters were waiting for us in the lobby like a pack of hungry wolves. We walked right by them, ignoring their clamoring requests for comment. Marya Fyodorovna strode by them to the lift, her head held high, her carriage proud and dignified. Maxim gave the reporters a crisp military salute, then blocked off their questions with an upraised hand.

In our rooms on the ninth floor, we found H. Gaylord Wilshire and Joseph Mandelkern anxiously awaiting our return. Their news was worse than that of the newspapers. We had been requested to leave the premises of the Hotel Belleclaire.

"Roblee, the manager is intransigent." Mr. Wilshire explained. "He feels the public outcry against Maxim and Mrs. Gorki will damage the hotel's reputation and therefore its business."

"Business." Gorki sniffed. "Let me talk to him about business."

"No, Maxim," Mr. Mandelkern advised. "It will do no good now. This Roblee has publicly stated his intention to have you find other lodgings. He made a grand pronouncement to the press that he could not 'tolerate the presence of persons whose character has been questioned' or some such drivel as that. He was indignant and self-righteous."

"We did our best to dissuade him," Mr. Wilshire added. "He was quite adamant."

"The bloody hypocrite," Maxim said. "How does a glorified innkeeper presume to pass such judgments on other people? Who does he imagine himself to be, the arbiter of taste for the entire city, country?"

"Nevertheless," Mr. Wilshire said, "we must move you out of here."

"Outrageous," Gorki said. "A dirty, slimy scandal."

"Please, Maxim," Mr. Wilshire said, "come stay with me and my wife. It will get you out of the public eye and avoid further negative publicity. At least for today."

"No," Maxim replied sternly. "I will not hide from this storm. Marya Fyodorovna is my wife. No law devised or made by man could make her any more so. It is a base calumny to suggest otherwise. Never was a union more holy than that between she and I. I will prepare a statement that says so for the American press by later today. Mr. Mandelkern may I impose on you to help relocate us?"

"Well, yes. We can try the Lafayette-Brevoort downtown. Perhaps they will be less 'nice' in their personal judgments."

"Very well," Maximovich said. "Let's get to it."

DISPOSSESSED—APRIL 14

WORD OF MAXIM'S "UNACCEPTABLE" RELATIONSHIP with Marya Fyodorovna moved through town nearly as fast as we did. We had barely gotten inside the Lafayette-Brevoort at Fifth Avenue and Eighth Street before its manager, a Mr. Lablancha, told us we were not welcome in his establishment. Mr. Mandelkern again took our part and wrested a concession from Lablancha to recommend us to the Rhinelander apartments across the street. This appeared to be a great boon and we thankfully took our belongings there. The Rhinelander manager, a Mr. Geraty, assigned us two suites, one on the sixth floor, the other on the eighth.

We settled in rather hurriedly as it was late in the day and we were expected at the Grand Central Palace for a socialist gathering and would later attend a performance by the Russian Players at the Lyceum. Maxim nonetheless made sure that the American press was fully advised of his position with regard to our "predicament."

"The publication of such a libel," he said, "is a dishonor to the American press. I am surprised that in a country famed for its love of fair play and reverence for women such a slander as this should have gained credence. I think that this dirt is conspired by friends of the current Russian government. I do not believe this disagreeable act could have come from the American people. And to my enemies I say I am always strongest when I stand alone. The bitter cup contains the noblest wine of life, and I am not afraid to drain it. All is harmony in my soul. There is music in the air and an atmosphere of poetry all about."

With Maxim's brave words ringing in our ears, we went out for our evening engagements escorted by Joseph Mandelkern, Ivan Narodny, and several of our fellow Russian socialists. At both the Grand Central Palace and later at the Lyceum, where we saw our marvelous Russian Players, Maxim and Marya Fyodorovna in particular received a loud, long, and warm welcome.

It was as if our friends—and we still had many—wanted to tell all of the city, all of America, that the moral judgments and condemnation of Maxim and Marya was narrow, illegitimate, and irrelevant. Gorki was a great writer, revolutionist, and man. The particular circumstances of his domestic life were of absolutely no importance in the grand scheme of things.

When we left the Lyceum, around midnight, the day's earlier nastiness had worn off to some degree, muted by the pleasantness of our evening's activities. As we drove back to our apartments with restored spirits we were still hopeful for our American fund-raising mission. The moment we entered the Rhinelander, however, all was bluntly dashed, as the new American reality waited for us in the form of our luggage, which was piled neatly in the lobby.

"What is this?" Marya Fyodorovna demanded of the manager.

"It is your party's luggage, madame." He came around from behind the lobby counter. "Or should I say mademoiselle?"

"You should say, madame." Marya talked to the man as if he were an unmanageable child. "And I want to know why our things are out here in the lobby?"

"I am afraid, madame—and sir." Geraty turned to face Maxim, who suddenly appeared nervous when the man's sharp English was aimed at him. I translated for Maxim as rapidly as I could. "Given the current circumstances of your personal arrangements, Mrs. Kelly, the proprietor of these apartments, has insisted that you find lodgings elsewhere."

"Oh, she has, has she?" Marya snapped. "You miserable shadow of a man, how dare you and your despicable 'proprietor' judge mine and my husband's relationship? How dare you throw us out into the night with not so much as a notice of any kind? You and your establishment are the most onerous of all things in a city that I now see is inhabited only by the lowest of hypocritical, self-righteous worms. How dare you, indeed."

"Nonetheless, madame, monsieur," Geraty responded haughtily. "I must insist that you and your party vacate the premises forthwith."

"Forthwith my foot," Marya Fyodorovna cried. "You hateful man."

"Please, my dear." Maxim took his wife's arm. "There's nothing left for it. We must find another place."

"But… Maxim."

"Come. We will find other lodgings." Then to Geraty he said, which I again interpreted, "Can you please get a car here for us, and for our things?"

"At once, sir." Geraty turned from me to Maxim and bowed courteously.

"Here Nikolai Evgenevich," Gorki said, "stay with my wife for a moment please. And Zinka, help the manager with the baggage and make sure everything is here."

"Yes, father," Zinka said dutifully.

I took Marya by the arm and led her to a couch where she sat down and held her head in her hands. Maxim, seemingly oblivious to us all now, walked out the glass front door and stood on the sidewalk just beyond, his head held high, his shoulders thrust up and back in a manner suggesting pride and dignity even at a time of personal resignation. He waited there by himself until the car arrived for our luggage.

––––––––––––

REACTION AND RESPONSE—APRIL 15

DESPITE BEING HURT BY MAXIM'S rejection of the offer to stay at his home during our current lodging crisis, H. Gaylord Wilshire reappeared and found us a place to stay after we were removed from the Rhinelander. Mr. Wilshire also helped us find Mr. and Mrs. Joseph Martin, who graciously offered us exile in their home on Staten Island. Mr. Wilshire seemed overjoyed to have reconciled with Maxim and we breakfasted at the Lafayette-Brevoort—the second hotel from which we had been ejected the day before—where Maxim grilled Mr. Wilshire, through me, about public reaction to our situation.

"What about Twain and Howells? Surely they defended me, did they not? And what of our fund-raising efforts, are they damaged beyond repair?"

"I wish, Maxim," Mr. Wilshire said, "that I had better news, but you already know most of what's been said in today's papers."

"Yes, yes, right next to the story of the Negroes being burned in Missouri. Read it, Nikolai Evgenevich."

"*The Times* says '*Gorki and Actress Asked To Quit Hotel.*' *The Sun* says the *'purity of our inns is threatened.*'"

"Ridiculous, of course," Mr. Wilshire said, "but as for Twain and Howells ... well, that's public record now also. Howells has taken the coward's path and refused any comment whatsoever, and Twain—the great 'revolutionist' as he likes to color himself—now says that your 'efficiency as a persuader is seriously impaired' perhaps even destroyed by your violation of certain 'laws of conduct.'"

"The miserable bourgeois hack," Maxim said bitterly.

"It is almost certain," Mr. Wilshire said, "that he and Howells will resign as your literary sponsors and cancel all the scheduled fundraisers we had planned."

"You have more from the great Twain?" Maxim saw me point to yet another passage in the Times. "Read it to them and then translate for me."

"It says here that Maximovich has violated 'custom' which is worse than violating the law because 'law is only sand while custom is custom; it is built of brass, boiler iron, granite; facts, reasonings, arguments have no more effect upon it than the idle winds have upon Gibraltar.'"

"Absurd hyperbole," Mr. Martin commented.

"A self-serving, cowardly, prude's way out," Marya Fyodorovna said.

"Remarkable, isn't it?" Mr. Martin observed. "That the gentlemen and ladies who supported revolution in Russia, bloody or otherwise, just two days ago are so appalled by a simple matrimonial irregularity that they will now deny Mr. Gorki, the renowned spokesman for that same revolution, as if he had become a pariah."

"What about the other cities we had planned to visit?" Maxim said. "Chicago, Boston?"

"In all candor, Maxim," Mr. Wilshire said, "they do not seem well disposed to receiving you after this, uh, flap."

"Perhaps we should return to Europe?" I suggested.

"No." Marya was firm. "We came to America as much for Maximovich's health as for the bloody revolution. Perhaps there is some other place, somewhere where we can stay that is out of the way. Somewhere Maxim could restore his health and continue his work and writing without the distractions of this fiasco."

"My writing, or I should say my commitment to writing, is as responsible for our predicament as anything else," Maxim said.

"I'm afraid you may be right." Mr. Wilshire concurred, to our surprise. "It appears that when the other papers learned you had signed exclusively with the Hearst papers, their jealousy and ire was aroused. The newspaper business, especially here in New York is highly competitive—to use a clean term—and it was Hearst's rival, Mr. Pulitzer's World, that broke the relationship between yourself and Mrs. Gorki."

"All the more reason to get away from here," Marya said.

"If it wouldn't seem too forward of me," Mr. Martin said. "My wife and I have a retreat home in the Catskill Mountains. We would be more than happy to have you as our guests there. We seldom get the opportunity to use it ourselves, so you would be undisturbed most of the time. I mean, of course, if such an arrangement would suit you."

Maxim looked at Marya and she nodded her head. With a broad smile and a big sigh, Maximovich stood and came around the table to Mr. Martin.

"Thank you, my friend." He said through me, pumping Mr. Martin's hand over and over and hugging him several times until the gentleman became embarrassed. "Thank you from the bottom of my heart. And thank you also," Maxim added with a sweep of his arm that took in the rest of us at the table, "for all of us."

Mr. Wilshire coughed, Maxim and Marya Fyodorovna exchanged a warm embrace, and I signaled the waiter to bring another round of tea. It promised to be another lovely spring day in New York and we raised our cups to the hope of a better, perhaps more tranquil, future in America.

———————

AFTERMATH—APRIL TO SEPTEMBER, 1906

AFTER OUR NEW YORK CITY experience, the Catskills were nearly idyllic. Maxim made a few more attempts at fundraising, going to Philadelphia and even making the delayed trip to Boston, but they were of little use. The New York debacle left him a persona non-grata in post-Victorian American society—especially in mainstream literary circles.

Despite this, he was happy. His health improved, and he began to work again, hard and steady. He read and wrote for hours at a stretch and produced two of his greatest works, the play, *Enemies*, and the working-class novel *Mother*. He also corresponded with other writers and revolutionists. It was a regime that would have exhausted a far healthier man.

To express his disappointment over the failure of our mission to America and to recoup some of the money he had hoped to raise, Maxim also wrote many articles and essays for pay in American newspapers and magazines. In these, he took American capitalistic excesses to task. He found it both ironic and humorous that the same people he criticized so openly were willing, even happy, to pay for the right to publish that criticism. It was one of the aspects of democratic capitalism that Maxim found most fascinating and simultaneously repulsive.

Gorki also battled publisher Randolph Hearst, who still printed Maxim's essays but didn't pay for them. And when Marya Fyodorovna's health weakened after many harsh and personal attacks on her in the American papers, Gorki struck back with a vengeance.

He wrote the essay "City of the Yellow Devil" and called the people of New York ignorant and barbaric. The article came out in late summer and generated yet another storm of virulent assaults on Maxim and the revolution. Describing New Yorkers as slaves to the yellow devil that is capitalist greed, Maxim's piece provoked more than twelve hundred objections from its readers and many cries for his deportation from the country.

Our weakening economic and social prospects were dealt a final blow when we learned that Maxim's little daughter, Katia, had died during August in Russia. Gathering our things together and bidding farewell to those who helped us during our troubled stay, we spent September in preparation for our departure.

At the first opportunity in early October, on a fine, crisp day, we left America, going first to Germany then on to the warm and healthy atmosphere of Capri. Our American adventure was over. Maxim had come as a conquering hero, been reviled as an immoral anarchist, then denied by the people who had ardently clamored for his presence in that young and enigmatic land. Although Maximovich's reputation as a great writer and international figure only grew brighter through the subsequent years—even in the United States—he was never to set foot on American soil again. Ever.

CLICK IT OR TICKET

OUT OF OLD, PARANOID HABIT, Billy Frank Thompson checked his rear view mirror. He had been stopped by the police so many times in his life that being pulled over, as was happening now for the first time in a long time, had once been almost a daily ritual. But not anymore. After his second stint in the Arizona State Penitentiary in Florence, he saw the light.

He read a prison library book account of how Oklahoma City bomber Timothy McVeigh had been caught because the police had initially pulled him over for not having a license plate on his purported getaway car. That was when his epiphany occurred. It was more of a modest realization, actually.

Reduced to its lowest common denominator, the sudden understanding went as follows—if you looked like a regular guy, spent money like a regular guy, paid your bills and your house payment on time and kept your car in basic, street legal condition, well, you were a regular guy and, if you acted calm, cool, and not unfriendly, any contact with the authorities would go much better. It really was a simple idea.

Now, on a typically hot and frantic TGI Friday afternoon, with traffic picking up on the surface streets of Phoenix, he glanced at the registration and insurance forms held behind clear plastic in the cloth-covered cardboard holder attached to the sun visor above the driver's seat in his seven-year-old Honda Accord. Everything was in order, even if the insurance form was faked by an old buddy of his from Florence. The cops never called in on insurance forms. The new registration year sticker was clean and clearly visible on the back plate and his driver's license was current and up to date. Everything was squared away.

He coolly turned the Accord into the first side street he could and, making sure he had signaled properly, pulled over to the curb at a safe distance from the corner. He was a stickler for these little details. It went down well with the police.

Still, for all his preparation, he had a moment's terror when he looked in his outside mirror and saw the police officer get out of his patrol car and walk toward him. But the fear passed quickly as he reminded himself that, other than the .38 caliber six-shot revolver in the console and the nearly one pound bag of weed tucked under the spare tire wheel well in the trunk—which he was taking over to his recently paroled yard buddy, Leo Hankins—he was as legit as anybody else on the roads. But he also knew better than to reach for any of his documents before the policeman requested them. They always wanted to see your hands clearly at all times. He put his hands on the steering wheel in plain sight.

"Good afternoon," the policeman, a barrel-chested, thick-bodied man with muscles like an NWO wrestler, said.

"Good afternoon." Billy Frank replied pleasantly.

He did not smile, and he did not intend to act overly friendly. Strict professionalism was always best when dealing with the John Laws.

"Do you know why I stopped you today, sir?"

"Uh, no I don't... Officer Lesner."

"Have you heard of our 'Click It or Ticket' program, sir?"

"I believe I have. Having to do with buckling up, isn't it?"

"That's exactly correct, sir. Our 'Click It or Ticket' program is among the finest in the nation. We have a high rate of compliance among our citizens, and fatalities and injuries are down, which is the purpose of the program."

Sure it is, Billy Frank thought to himself, while unselfconsciously running his right hand up and down his secured seat belt, *you guys really give a crap whether anybody lives or dies.* Not likely. It's all about insurance company profits, not about people's safety. Stupid insurance companies. All they want is for us to pay and pay and for them to never pay out.

The world was full of insurance rules, he groused in his own mind, lessons learned from the Einstein of Florence, Charles McKinney, better known in the joint as C-Mac. Helmets on children riding bikes in suburban neighborhoods where their biggest danger was missing lunch because they had ridden over to the public swimming pool too late in the morning to make it back home for momma's food. Rollerbladers wearing more protective gear than soldiers in combat, car airbags that went off if you bumped into anything, much less hit it hard—and they exploded out so fast they could kill a kid. Yeah, they care about us all right.

"That's great," he heard himself say out loud to the officer.

"Well, sir, I'm glad to see that you are buckled in properly. Safe and secure. We're stopping cars at random today to make sure citizens are being safe, and you passed the test."

"Excellent,"

"Have a good day, then, sir." The policeman stepped back from the car.

"That's all?"

"That's all. We appreciate your cooperation."

"Thank you, officer. You have a good day, too."

The policeman snapped a sharp salute and then walked back to his cruiser. Billy Frank watched him until he was back in the police vehicle. After a moment, while he watched to see if the policeman was going to call in his plates, which he didn't seem to, he flipped on his left signal light and pulled safely back onto the street. When he rounded the next corner and out of sight of the police car, he let loose with a whoop and a happy laugh.

"Damn I'm good," he said. "I have got this thing down."

LEO HANKINS LIVED IN TEMPE, in an old house near the corner of Priest and University on the city's northwest edge—edge, that is, if it hadn't been for the constant forty-plus year squeeze together of all the little towns in the valley into the monstrous megalopolis thing that greater Phoenix had become.

Billy Frank pulled the Honda up to the curb in front of the house, switched off the engine and, after taking the .38 out of the console and sliding it into the waistband of his trousers, stepped out into the sizzling Phoenix heat. He adopted a casual attitude as he walked to the back of the car and opened the trunk. He could've used the trunk opener beside the front seat but didn't want any prying eyes to see in the back until he got there himself.

The weed was in a small sport bag squished under the spare tire and Billy Frank gingerly removed it. He was always surprised at how much weed weighed. It was like no other plant matter he could imagine. He guessed it weighed so much because so much was involved in its growing, purchasing, selling, and distributing. The bag he used for carrying his stashes always felt its best, and lightest, right after he had delivered its contents to whoever was buying. Like Leo today.

"Yo, dude," Leo called from the front door.

He had apparently been watching for the arrival of his weed. Billy Frank headed up the sidewalk to the house.

"Have any trouble findin' the place?" Leo opened the door.

"Nah, piece a cake."

Inside, the house was a mess. Leo's girlfriend was a stripper in a club down on Van Buren and she usually made the living while Leo stayed home getting drunk or stoned and hanging with his ex-con pals. Nobody seemed to be concerned about housework, like washing dishes, vacuuming the floor, picking up dirty clothes and so forth.

Billy Frank pushed some underwear out of the way with his shoes and tossed the bag of weed onto a beer can, ashtray, and paper plate covered coffee table. A small Styrofoam container flew onto the floor, but Leo ignored it as he sat down on the edge of a dirty, cluttered, and worn couch. Billy Frank pushed some more clothes off a plastic chair and sat down across the coffee table from Leo.

"So you got it, huh?" Leo's eyes lit up with excitement.

"I got it."

"Primo?"

"Nothin' but."

"How much?"

"I'll take thirteen hundred for the bag. Or a mix. Cash, rock, maybe you got some weapons?"

"That's kind of steep, ain't it? Is it a full pound?"

"Steep? Are you kiddin' me? You can double that around here by the bag. Make even more by the quarter. How long you been out of the joint?"

"Just askin', that's all."

"Sure it's a pound." Billy Frank knew it was at least one lid shy of a pound. He had given that to a dancer in a club for a few favors.

"Okay, I got some dough. I got a couple of semis you might like."

"Let's see 'em."

AFTER CONCLUDING THEIR BUSINESS, LEO had come up with $650 in cash and two police-type .9mm Glocks, the two old cellmates drove back into town to a strip club where Leo's girlfriend did not work. Over shots of tequila and whiskey with beer chasers, the two ex-cons reminisced about the good old days in Florence.

"I never forget ole C-Mac." Leo sucked on a Pacifico beer. "What a dude."

"Crazy son bitch," Billy Frank said, as his favorite girl in the club came up for yet another lap dance. He'd had five already and the girl was really starting to get him worked up.

"Yeah, that plan of his to smoke until he got lung cancer and then sue the tobacco companies. Man, that's crazy. But probably crazy enough to work."

"Crazy enough to get him dead if you ask me." Billy Frank eased his hips against the dancer's muscular buttocks. "What you gonna do with millions of bucks when you're dead?"

"He could buy new lungs with all that dough. Sure enough."

Billy Frank moaned as the girl ground down into his groin.

"That C-Mac," Leo continued his euphoric recall of his recent state pen days, "he was some smart cookie, though."

"Oof."

"'Member how he told us all about politics, man, and how everything works out here in the world? Man, he knew his stuff."

"Yeah."

"I remember," Leo said with a sparkle in his drunk eyes, "C-Mac told us that the insurance companies owned America, man. That they took everybody's money and made everybody into wimps. Remember that?"

"Uh."

"Lawyers, too. They rule the country. All the politicians, he told us, they're all lawyers. I mean, after all, politics is about laws, he said, you know? C-Mac always said, 'Look at your politicians. Where do they come from? Law firms, country clubs, chambers of commerce. You think they give a damn about anybody but their own kind. Not likely. Not regular guys. And sure, not us cons.' Man, he knew his stuff."

"Ungh."

"And he used to really get wound up about 9/11. He hated all the rules they put in after that. He said that Homeland Security thing sounded like Germany back there when they called it the Fatherland or some such crap. I can't remember all he said. He was one sharp dude."

"Why don't you shut up about C-Mac," Billy Frank said as the girl pummeled his crotch with her own. "Get you a girl or something. I'm busy."

"Oh, yeah, sorry, man."

Leo watched the girl working out on his old cellmate for a moment, then waved a twenty-dollar bill toward the elevated dance floor for a woman of his own. A dark-haired girl saw the twenty and came hustling over.

"That's more like it," Billy Frank said, when the dark-haired girl had started working out on Leo. "To hell with thinkin' about the joint, this is where the action is."

"Yeah, man." Leo took a deep breath as the girl moved her buttocks into position over his crotch. "You got that right."

———————

"I GOT ONE PROBLEM." BILLY Frank told Leo as the two of them continued to drink their tequila shots with Pacifico chasers.

"What's that, man?" Leo slurred.

He had been used to joint gin so long that real booze was knocking him for a loop.

"My old woman."

"Oh, yeah, Sherry or something."

"Cheryl and her dumbass kid."

"Dumbass kid," Leo repeated blankly.

"Richard Lee, and he ain't even my kid. He's some dumb-ass cracker, trailer park butthole's kid. But she's still after me for alimony and child support. What a bitch."

"Bitch."

"I'm gonna pay her a visit tomorrow. Gonna straighten her out."

"That's the way," Leo said. "Don't take no bull."

"I ain't in the joint no more. I don't have to take nothing off anybody."

"Don't have to." Leo did his repeating thing.

"As long as I play the game right, look the part, I'm all right."

"Right on."

Billy Frank ordered one more round of tequila and beer and then suggested that they head back to Leo's.

"What for?"

"Your girl will be home maybe by then. Call her and have her bring a friend home."

"What?" Leo tried to shake the alcohol fog from his brain.

"I got money. I don't mind payin' for it."

"Oh, sure. I'll give her a buzz on my cell."

"Do that now."

After Leo made the hookup with his girl and they finished a last round, the boys left the club. Out in the parking lot, they smoked some more weed before heading back to Tempe. While they were doing the doobie, an old drunk staggered out of the club and walked toward them. The man wobbled, barely able to stand. His car was two over from Billy Frank's and when the man opened his car door he fell into the front seat, out like a light.

"See that?" Billy Frank said to Leo.

"Stupid ass."

Billy Frank looked around the parking lot. There was no one around.

"Come on."

Leo tagged along as they hustled over to the passed out man.

"Get his billfold."

"Got it." Leo quickly found the billfold inside the drunk's coat pocket.
"Look how much."

They took the money and tossed the billfold back down on the passed out man.

"Not bad." Billy Frank did a quick count.

"Yeah?"

"Yeah. Close to three fifty."

"Three dollars? I thought he looked—"

"Three hundred and fifty, you dope, get it together."

"Cool, man," Leo said.

ON THE WAY BACK TO Tempe, Billy Frank went through seven pieces of gum trying to get the alcohol off his breath just in case they might have a chance encounter with the law. Leo insisted on chewing one piece, but Billy Frank wouldn't let him have any more.

"I'm the designated driver. You just sit there and shut up if we get stopped. You can be drunk. I can't. Even if I am."

"Cool." Leo closed his eyes and leaned his head back against the seat.

And sure enough, down near where Van Buren and Washington come together and become Mill Avenue going into Tempe, they saw flashing lights and a whole raft of police cars.

"Hell, a DUI roadblock. Wouldn't you know it."

"What?" Leo roused for the moment.

"Just relax." Billy Frank popped two more pieces of a sweet, minty gum into his mouth. "I'll handle it. Just sit there and don't say anything."

"You should've taken Fortieth or Forty-Eighth. The back way."

"This'll be fine. Just relax."

Billy Frank eased up on the Honda's accelerator but made sure he didn't approach the checkpoint too slowly. That was a dead giveaway to the cops, too. Drive normal, act normal. Like you were coming home from visiting a friend somewhere.

"Good evening, sir." A young policeman of medium height and build came up to the driver's side of the Honda. He looked into the vehicle, checked the backseat and then looked over at Leo. "You fellows been out drinking?"

"We were visiting friends, officer," Billy Frank said calmly, evenly. "My friend had a couple too many. I'm the designated driver."

"How about you, then? How many did you have?"

"None, sir."

"None?" A large, muscular policeman came up behind the young officer.

"What's up, Jackson?" the big officer said.

"These two guys...." Officer Jackson began.

"Officer Lesner." Billy Frank practically cried out.

"Good evening, sir." Officer Lesner stepped up alongside the Honda.

"Remember me?"

"Yes, sir. How are you, sir?"

"I'm fine. You're working long hours I see."

"Doing a twelve on, twelve off shift."

"Man, that's a lot of hours. Tiring, huh?"

"Not too bad."

"We should probably check them or move them on out," Officer Jackson suggested. "There's a line forming up."

"All right," Officer Lesner said. "Your partner there certainly looks inebriated. You driving him home?"

"That's exactly what I'm doing, officer. My buddy Leo and me were at a friend's party tonight and he had a few too many. As I told the other officer, I'm the designated driver."

"Check 'em or let 'em go." Officer Jackson leaned back from the vehicle. He waved at some other officers in the roadblock.

"You haven't been drinking yourself?" Officer Lesner said.

"No, sir. I'm the designated driver."

Officer Lesner looked around. The line of cars behind the Honda was getting long. The other officers held up their hands as if to say what's up. Officer Lesner leaned back down to the window of the Honda.

"All right then, sir. Go on ahead. Drive safely and remember to never drink and drive."

"You bet, sir. Good night to you, Officer Lesner."

"Good night, sir." Officer Lesner moved back and motioned them on.

Billy Frank drove on with a wave back for the officers. Leo sat up his seat and howled.

"Damn, Billy Frank," The ex-jailbird yelled. "You've really got it together."

———————————

HE WOKE TO BRIGHT SUNLIGHT in his eyes and a painful headache. Leo's girlfriend's girlfriend was beside him on the living room couch, naked except for a silver choker chain around her smooth neck. He extracted an arm from under the girl and slowly sat up. The girl moaned lowly and turned on the couch. Her body was twisted around with arms and legs flopped everywhere but her naked breasts stood straight up.

The wonders of silicone, Billy Frank thought, running his fingers over each breast in turn.

"Oh, baby," the girl said, not really awake.

"Just relax."

The girl briefly opened her eyes, then went back to sleep, pulling a pillow around her for cover.

Gingerly, Billy Frank got up and went into the bathroom to take a shower.

———————————

ON HIS WAY OVER TO his ex-wife's house on Twenty-Eighth just north of McDowell, Billy Frank medicated his headache with a couple of aspirins and a hit or two from a stray roach he'd found in Leo's living room. He had taken what was left of Leo's bag of weed just to have something for later and was reflective, even contemplative as he drove.

Like most everyone else in the United States, he—sitting with a room full of fellow prisoners—had watched the television coverage of the events unfolding so horrendously in New York City on September 11, 2001. The attacks on the World Trade Center had saddened and sickened Billy Frank. So much so, that if he had been eligible, he would have joined the U.S. Army on the spot to fight the perpetrators of such a heinous act of war.

Also, like most everyone else in the United States, he—at that point not one of the great thinkers in the prison—believed what he was told on television and was in favor of all measures that were introduced to control these attacks on Americans and American soil.

He approved of the war in Afghanistan, he favored armed air marshals on every plane flight, the passing of the Patriot Act, and he cheered the creation of the Department of Homeland Security program and its head, Tom Ridge—approved these moves that is, until he got paroled in early summer 2002 and had to begin readjusting to civilian life.

What he found, as he tried to blend back into civilian life in Phoenix, the only town in the state where he felt he could find the anonymity he craved, was that the Patriot Act in general and what he saw as its more specific direct and indirect applications were having a bone chilling impact on the freedoms that most Americans had once taken for granted.

Now, people could be rousted out for basically no reason and held without charge for whatever amount of time the authorities deemed appropriate. Mostly this harassed Muslim-Americans and Americans of Arab descent, but Billy Frank—as a man who needed freedom to pursue his primary occupations of thief and drug runner—saw the new clampdown in a more personal way.

What bothered him the most was the increase in police presence in general. There seemed to be cops everywhere now. And they were always stopping you for no good reason. One day it would be a roadblock to check for traffic violations, on the weekends it would be one for DUIs, and of late, roadblocks to see if you were wearing your seat belt or not.

His old yard buddy C-Mac in Florence had been the first to turn him on to this way of thinking and now sometimes he wished C-Mac would've kept his yap shut. Except for being the triggering mechanism of his own awakening on to how to avoid hassles with the authorities. Now that was something that had been worthwhile learning.

Turning east off Twenty-Seventh at McDowell, he made an immediate left up Twenty-Eighth and soon found Cheryl's place. He knew he was going to be violating a restraining order in going to see her but having completed his parole several months ago he would not automatically go back to jail for doing so. He had a bone or two to pick with his ex and he didn't give a damn about any restraining order. Who the hell was gonna stop him from crossing it anyway?

"What the hell are you doing here?" Cheryl yelled when she answered the door bell. She made no effort to open the screen door between herself and him.

"We need to talk."

"There's nothin' to talk about. If you don't go I'll call the cops."

"Call 'em." He tried the screen door. It was locked. "Open this door."

"No."

For a moment he stared through the screen at his ex-wife. She looked the same. Tall, thin, dishwater blonde hair. He couldn't tell for sure but maybe her mouth was still a little puffy on the right side from the last time they'd gotten together. She was wearing a ratty green night gown that looked like it had been cut from a wallpaper design and, despite her fear of him, she also had that defiant, disrespectful look on her face that he had grown to hate. With one hard shove he knocked the screen door open and stalked into the house.

She cried and ran back into the center of the cluttered, toy-strewn living room. Her little boy, Richard Lee, hovered by a once white, torn couch at the back of the room. The child had been fathered by a co-worker of hers down at the Salt River Project offices where she was a mail clerk—while Billy Frank was in Florence.

"This ain't gonna take long, bitch." Billy Frank threatened. Richard Lee started to cry. "Shut that little asshole up." The boy ran to his mother who held him tight against her.

"You get outta here."

"I'm gonna make this easy. Drop this alimony and child support crap that's eatin' all my income up and you'll never see me again."

"We need that money, you owe it to us."

"I don't owe you nothing. That little son of a bitch ain't even mine. Who is the father of that little turd anyway?"

"He's yours."

"Bull, I was in the pen. Nice try."

"The court ruled...."

"The court can go to hell."

"I'll call the police. They'll put you back in."

"Call 'em," he yelled. He hated threats. From his yardbird experience, he felt a man had to respond to every one of them.

"I'm going to." Cheryl held the crying Richard Lee and picked up a cell phone.

"Put that down." He stepped forward and slapped the phone away. It crashed across the room, back cover flying off. Richard Lee let out a wail. "Shut him up."

"Leave us alone. Get out."

"Not till you promise to drop this money crap."

"I won't. We need that money."

"So you and your punk ass lover can keep makin' a fool of me? Say you're gonna drop the alimony and the child support. Say it."

"No."

"Damn you."

"Go to hell."

That was all he could take. He lunged forward and hit Cheryl. Hit her hard with his closed fist. In the mouth, same as the last time. She shrieked and fell back, bouncing off the couch. The little boy fell to the floor howling. He advanced toward the child with an upraised hand. The boy screamed and ran. Cheryl tried to struggle up but Billy Frank cuffed her across the head. Blood from a cut on her swollen lip splattered lightly on the floor. She stopped then and curled up into a fetal ball by the couch, crying inconsolably. He checked his right hand. The middle knuckle was torn and slightly bleeding.

"Just drop it." He eased toward the front door, shaking his cut hand. "You know I mean business. And you know I'll find you if you try to move. Drop it now."

To the sounds of the child crying in a back room and Cheryl sobbing by the couch, he turned and walked out the door, slamming it as he went. The door banged shut but bounced right back open, the latch having been broken when he first stormed into the house.

Outside, he calmly got into the Honda, made a U-turn in front of Cheryl's house and headed back down toward McDowell.

LATE IN THE AFTERNOON AFTER he had paid his ex-wife a visit, Billy Frank found himself aimlessly driving around. Avoiding the busy expressways around town, he had driven up and down Central from Washington to Camelback several times just wasting time. Finally he got hungry, found a greasy spoon and ate a late lunch.

Feeling refreshed after the meal, he decided to pay Leo another visit and see if his old pal maybe wanted to hit the clubs again today and pick up on another couple of babes. Heading out Van Buren toward Tempe, he had made it almost to Twenty-Fourth when he saw the traffic ahead slowing up.

"What the hell now?" He pounded the steering wheel with his right hand. "Ow." His cut middle knuckle was still a little bloody, and sore.

What the hell now turned out to be yet another police roadblock. This time a seat belt check. He sighed, braked the Honda, and sucked the dried blood on his knuckle. When he got up to where the police were actually checking each driver to see if they were buckled in, he could not believe his eyes.

"Officer Lesner?" He said when the big policeman strode up to his car.

"Hello again, sir."

"This is amazing." He made sure the policeman could not see his scraped up knuckle. "Three times in just over a day. Do you ever get any time off?"

"Yes, sir. Just came back on duty a couple of hours ago. It's a busy time for us."

"I can see that."

"Well, sir, I can see that you are still a law-abiding citizen. Buckled in all safely and securely. We won't keep you any longer. I wish everyone else would follow the laws as strictly as you do, sir."

"Oh, yeah," he said without irony, but not missing it either. "I wish they would, too."

"Have a good day then, sir." Officer Lesner backed away from the Honda. "And good motoring to you."

"Thank you, officer. You have a nice day now."

"Thank you, sir."

On his way to Tempe, Billy Frank felt just grand. He still had the .38 in the console, the small bag of Leo's weed in his pocket, and he was sure he had Cheryl scared quiet. He knew some guys up in Paradise Valley who had some rock to move and that would make him a good buck or two. Things were going really well for him. And he owed it all to his moment of clarity in the state pen.

All the new rules were designed to freak out the average Joe or Jane, not guys like him. As long as he gave the appearance that he was a regular guy, the cops were not likely to come down on him just out of the blue. He liked the way things had been going in the country of late. Everybody was so wrapped up in a mindless conformity to minor rules that they couldn't see or tell the difference between anyone or anything that was actually dangerous and something that was completely trivial.

This made things easy for smart crooks as he now considered himself. America had become one big land of whiners, weenies, and wimps. Billy Frank thought that was a good deal. He wanted it to stay that way as long as he lived.

OUT IN THE COUNTY

BOBBY EARL BUNTON DECIDED TO stop making crystal meth and just use it after his cousin, Tommy Ray Wilson, caught on fire when his trailer lab in the woods northwest of Fort Smith blew up on him. Tommy Ray came barreling out of the trailer screaming bloody murder with his wife Verleen chasing after him cursing and howling. She thought she was throwing water on Tommy Ray from a cup she had but it was some kind of flammable liquid and just made things worse.

"Damn you, Verleen," Tommy Ray screeched at his thick-bodied wife as he rolled across the front lawn fully ablaze.

"Tuck and roll you son of a bitch, tuck and roll," Verleen swore at her combusted partner.

Tommy Ray rolled, all right. In fact, he was flinging himself around the front yard like a chicken recently relieved of its head. After a few agonizing moments, he did manage to put out the fire. He stood up carefully and slowly, wisps of smoke trailing into the clear Arkansas air like little blue funnel clouds.

"Tuck and roll," was the first thing he thought to say to Verleen after he was no longer aflame. "Tuck and roll? That's what you do to the inside of a car, you dumb bitch. It's drop and roll. *Drop and roll.* I was on fire, not being upholstered."

"You knowed what I meant."

"Yeah."

When Tommy Ray told Bobby Earl about the incident, Bobby Earl immediately swore off of meth production forever.

"Hell," Tommy Ray said, "it was just a accident. Coulda happened to anybody. Ain't no reason to stop makin' up batches."

But Bobby Earl was adamant. He might be dumb but he wasn't stupid. He'd had enough of the smelly, dangerous chemicals and the fret and worry of buying too much of this or too much of that at the drug stores all over most of Crawford County, as well as southern Washington and western Franklin Counties. No, he would stick to using booger and leave the cooking to amped up nut jobs like his not-flame proof cousin.

"You gotta pay for it from here on in." Tommy Ray warned.

"I reckon then that's what I'll do." Bobby Earl had no idea how he would afford it but by God he would somehow.

"Suit yourself."

"I will."

It didn't take long to realize he couldn't afford to buy the crank he used to help make. Tommy Ray was a hard ass about the price, and so Bobby Earl slowly drifted away from that scene. He moved south, into Fort Smith itself, looking for a connection and a cheap ass place to crash. Being a young man of a resourceful nature, he soon had found both.

He shacked up with a teenage runaway in a crappy trailer at a crappy park at the edge of town and spent his days alternately scuffling for drug money and getting high. Sometimes he would go as far as to cross the border into Oklahoma looking for scores and ways to raise cash, but he got busted for possession in some damned Okie town and spent a couple of months in their lousy creep-infested jail before his runaway girlfriend managed to bail him out. Of course he immediately jumped bail and headed back to Arkansas, putting a hard stop to his more overt activities in the Sooner State.

Sticking closer to home after the out of state bust, he discovered that he had a natural gift for breaking and entering. This made his nights a lot more entertaining than sitting around loaded watching television with his boring teenie-bopper girlfriend, who by then considered him to be just as boring. Instead, he would take off after dark and tell the girl he was going to the store for smokes.

Of course, he spent the entire evening carefully breaking back room windows, jiggling weak locks, and creepy crawling houses while he made off with anything he could find that wasn't nailed down and was worth something—anything. He wouldn't come back home until daylight but the girl would be asleep and she didn't seem to care whether he was there or not.

Unfortunately, one evening a late-returning family caught him robbing them and the old man of the house hog-collared Bobby Earl and held him until the police arrived. He was put in the Sebastian County jail and spent his days cleaning up the streets of Fort Smith in his prison jumpsuit.

Several weeks into his sentence, he heard of a program that would get him out of jail for a couple of hours a week. Every Wednesday night, the best-behaved prisoners could get a two-hour furlough to a local church. All you had to do was stay out of trouble for a week and feign an interest in religion and you were out of the county slam long enough to get some decent food and mingle with real live people instead of the losers he spent his days with picking up paper and junk along the roads in town and out in the county.

One night at the church a long, stringy-haired girl came in toting a kid with her. Her name was Mary Beth and she was all about Jesus. Bobby Earl saw she was just right for him right away. She was wide in the hips but with a sweet face, and kind of dumb. Tailor-made for an aspiring crook like himself.

"My name's Bobby Earl." He sidled up beside her in the food line at the church.

"Hi, I'm Mary Beth and this is—"

"I seen ya right away." He flattered the shy girl and stood so close to her that he could hear her breathe. "I bet you's a good Christian girl, ain't ya?"

"I love the Lord."

"Me, too." He looked her up and down like she was a ticket out of Arkansas, which maybe she was. "Do you believe Jesus helps those who help themselves?"

"I believe the preacher done said something like that."

"Can I sit with you and your baby there at supper?"

"I reckon." She looked down at her feet. The baby girl nestled her little head against the warmth of her mama's shoulder.

"Do you take your baby there with you all the time... I mean, you got somebody to watch after her sometimes."

"I'm mostly with her." She gave him the once over. "But my Aunt Sally sometimes do watch her. Why you want to know?"

"No reason, just conversation, that's all."

OVER THE NEXT WEEKS, BOBBY Earl slowly and carefully cultivated her. He was on his best behavior, doing all the Jesus stuff he could at the church, acting like he liked the girl's damned little baby, and trying his best to finagle his way into Mary Beth's good graces. It turned out to be an easy job.

Seems that she was primed for being treated well. She had had an abusive uncle—Bobby Earl wasn't sure from her stories that the uncle wasn't the baby's daddy, but that didn't matter none to him—and she was mostly alone in the world except for the dumb Aunt Sally that watched the baby sometimes.

"If you could leave your little one with your aunt sometime." He suggested one Wednesday night after they had stopped at a convenience store where he bought his favorite food, a pack of pecan twirls, and a big Orange Slice. "Me and you could slip away from this here church and have us some good times."

"I don't know." She demurred, but he kept insisting, and the next Wednesday she showed up at church without her child.

"You're a good girl," he said, "and I'm a bad boy."

"I don't think so. I think you just need Jesus in your life."

"Yeah." He pulled out half of a doobie he had in his shirt pocket and lit it up right outside the church. "Jesus, you, and some tote."

Mary Beth didn't know what to make of his blasphemy, but she believed in the regenerative power of Jesus in this and the afterlife, and so she stayed with him. He was wild, all right, and sort of crazy, but with Jesus he could become a good man, a good provider for her and her baby.

"You do know my baby's name, don't you?" She said one day when he had talked her into going to her aunt's house to "borrow" her car for a run through Fort Smith.

"Sure I do. It's baby."

"Say it."

"C'mon, let's go downtown and get hooked up."

"You don't know it."

"I know who I am. I'm Pretty Boy Floyd, I'm John Dillinger, I'm a bad mother."

"You're just a boy." Mary Beth sighed. "And Jesus will make you whole someday. He'll fill you with love, and you'll be saved by his blood."

"Damn straight." He squared his shoulders. "His blood and my blood will set me free."

FIVE OR SIX MORE WEEKS of sneaking away from the church on Wednesdays later, Bobby Earl hatched a grand scheme.

"I got a idea," he told Mary Beth. "Let's borrow your aunt's car and get out of this crap town. Maybe go out to Arizona or New Mexico."

"Arizona?" She thought of carrying Marcie Kay, her baby, to some faraway place. "Ain't that a long way aways?"

"Shoot." He downed the last pecan twirl from a twin-pack and guzzled some Orange Slice after. He didn't have the slightest idea where Arizona was, much less how far away. "Cain't be but a day or two, we'd be right back. I swear on your Jesus."

"Don't swear, it ain't right."

"Shee-it."

"And what about Marcie Kay?"

"What about her?"

"I cain't just leave her."

"It'd just be for a couple of days. Your aunt won't mind. Won't mind no more than borrowin' this car that she don't ever use."

"I don't know."

Bobby Earl didn't say anything else for a few moments as he struggled to drive and simultaneously light a pipe that held what looked like a small piece of glass in its center. He took a deep draw of smoke from the burning pipe, his cheeks puffing out like a deranged chipmunk. In moments, the deranged look spread to his eyes and entire face.

"You're scarin' me." Mary Beth pulled away from him.

"Ah, hell. Let's go right now."

"I cain't do that, not now. I need to see my baby 'fore we go."

"Won't be hardly long till you see her." His eyes were as wild as a mad hatter's. "We be back in no time."

"Oh, baby, please."

"Hell, we already gone." He spotted an entrance ramp onto I-40 West. "We gonna blow through Oklahoma like Bonnie and Clyde. We're the second comin' of them two. We are goin' west, baby, praise Jesus."

"Don't you blaspheme now."

But she didn't say anything more about where they were going.

Beside her, Bobby Earl, sky high and wired to the core, rolled down his window and howled into the Arkansas air. "I'm Pretty Boy Floyd, I'm John Dillinger, and Goddamn it, me and my girl is the new Bonnie and Clyde."

"I wish you wouldn't take the Lord's name in vain. It ain't right."

"Oh, hell, baby." He rolled up the car window and leaned back in the driver's seat with a demented smile. "There's just no stoppin' me. I'm behind the wheel now, not your fairy boy Jesus. It's hell to pay for Arizona and good riddance to Arkansas."

He rolled the window down again and stuck his face into the wind. Mary Beth closed her eyes and prayed.

Bobby Earl squealed with delight. "I'm a free son-of-a-bitch. Cain't nobody stop me now, 'cept the devil himself, and I'll knock his ugly ass off if he tries. Right, baby?"

Mary Beth didn't say a word. The boy looked over at her and laughed. The laugh, if she had been able to recognize it, was the laugh of someone leaning well over the narrow ledge between reality and fantasy, between reason and madness, between simple criminality and murder.

It was getting late in the day as the car sped down I-40, heading for the Oklahoma line. This was it for the young couple's options. Bobby Earl had locked them into an uncertain, impulsive future. He was hell bent for the desert southwest. There was no turning back.

BAR HARBOR

"LISTEN, LOU." CHARLIE WOODRUFF LEANED back in his plush, brown leather New York City literary agent's office chair. "I think you just need a break. You've been in the city too long. You should get out of town for a while, go somewhere quiet and calm. Re-energize your batteries. That'll get the words flowing again."

"I didn't mean to stay here so long," Lou Decker, possibly Charlie's most promising new client, replied. "I was just supposed to come up to sign the book contracts and do a few readings and such. It's turned out to be a month-long ordeal."

"Ordeal perhaps, but a successful one, you must admit."

"Well…."

"Well, nothing, are you kidding? You've been the toast of the town. Radio, TV, literary get-togethers, you're the hottest thing, a shining star."

"Let's not get carried away." Lou said. "I'm not exactly on the *Times* Bestseller List yet."

"But you will be, you will be. Next book, guaranteed best seller. All you have to do is get going on it."

"Yeah, well, that's the problem, isn't it? I'm completely blocked. Nothing is happening. I can't even come up with a new idea. Maybe I should go back to Wisconsin. Home is probably better."

"Maybe, but hear me out. Have you ever been up to Maine? I mean along the coast?"

"No, I never have. But I've always wanted to. People say Maine is a really beautiful place."

"Exactly, and especially so on the coast. I'll get you transpo up to Portland, you rent a car and drive up the coast to Bar Harbor. It's really nice there. Stay a few days, turn off your phone, don't check your e-mail, and see if being up there doesn't get your juices flowing again."

"Words, juices, you'll have me pouring out books like water from a drain pipe."

"You'll do it?"

"Ah." Lou considered the idea for a few moments. "Why the hell not? What have I got to lose?"

"That's the spirit," Charlie said. "That's the ticket."

LOU LIKED PORTLAND, MAINE. IT was a nice combination of old and new architecture, old and new history, and it was a coastal city after all. He rented an inexpensive compact car at the airport and then checked into a conveniently located hotel not too far from downtown and the waterfront and quite near a mall where he picked up snacks and drinks to hold him for a couple of days. The weather turned out to be surprisingly cool for so early in September, in the Midwest it could still be quite hot around Labor Day, and so he bought a heavy pullover sweater for evenings and in anticipation of encountering even lower temperatures as he headed north up the coast.

On the day before the holiday, he took a self-guided tour of the town, walking around to some art and history museums and then stopping for a nice lunch at an open air restaurant. Late in the afternoon, he drove down to the port and took an inexpensive cruise around the bay, checking out the lovely homes on little islets jutting out into the water. It was all quite tranquil and relaxing, allowing him to take his mind off the stress of his recent sojourn in New York and to forget, at least for the moment, that his publishers were expecting another book from him in short order.

Tired but content, he returned to his hotel with plenty of time to pack his bags and get ready for the drive up the coast in the morning. Life wasn't all that bad, he reminded himself, even if he was beginning to feel his nearly four decades on this earth and even if he found himself alone again after a longish, complex relationship with a woman he had once actually considered marrying. Thinking of Carol, his ex-partner, caused him to sigh unbidden and to remember his agent Charlie's final admonition when he had visited him back in New York.

"Go off somewhere and write a story with a love interest. That'll get you off the schneid with the writing block. People like love stories. Readers like love stories. I know some magazine editors who would love to get a story from you like that. Besides, you can work out your memories that way. Isn't that what you writers do? Turn your lives into art."

"Something like that."

He didn't really think a love story was much up his alley these days or anything he had ever really been much interested in. They were always too mushy, too unrealistic. He liked to write what he called "realistic" fiction.

"Well, make it realistic." Charlie said. "Just write something for a larger audience. Don't pin yourself down. Don't limit the potential size of your readership. It's good business to reach as many people as possible."

"Yeah." He doubted he was the guy for that kind of writing. "Reach as many people as possible."

AFTER HAVING A LIGHT BREAKFAST at a restaurant near the hotel, Lou drove his rental car to I-295 and headed out of Portland. It was a cool, bright day with a high, deep blue sky—perfect for driving and seeing the beautiful Maine coast. Dropping off I-295 onto Highway 1, he took the exit to Freeport and spent the time to actually drive by the L. L. Bean store just because it was easy to find.

From Freeport he continued north through Brunswick and Camden and far up country until Highway 3 joined Highway 1, finally dropping south and easterly toward Bar Harbor. Near Bar Harbor he began looking for a place to stay and saw a couple of quaint travel courts but went on into town for a quick look-see. After a short walkabout in what he took to be Bar Harbor's downtown, he drove out to a pier he had seen advertised in a tourist brochure to check out prices and times for a whale watching trip he thought sounded like fun.

Stopping at a grocery for some basic food and snacking items, and then at a liquor store for a decently priced bottle of Pinot Noir, he took the highway back out of town to find lodging for the night. A few miles out of Bar Harbor he found the Hideaway Courts, exactly the kind of place he was hoping for.

The Hideaway consisted of maybe ten or so little individual cabins, arranged in a kind of extended rectangle. He took one that was a little set off from the others in the lower left-hand side of the court, closer to the highway but far enough away to not be disturbed by traffic noise.

Inside, the one-room cabin was quite small. A single bed took up most of the right side as you entered and a chair across from it left only a walking space to get to the back of the room where the bathroom and shower were. On the left as you came in, was a small desk and chair—perfect for writing he noted—and behind it a small kitchen with a little stove and refrigerator.

"Absolutely perfect." He deposited the perishable groceries and drinks in the refrigerator. "Just ideal."

After having a Swiss cheese sandwich with veggie beans for supper, he dug his laptop out of its carrying case, hooked up a small mouse he liked to use and then plugged the PC into a wall socket to save battery power. He had made some story notes on hotel paper back in Portland and found those, too, and entered them into Word.

"How people ever used to write by long hand or typewriter escapes me," he told the quiet little cabin. "Thank God for laptops and word processing.

"Woop," he said a couple of moments later, after entering most of his notes in a file. "Wine. Gotta have some wine. Can't be a writer in a little cabin on the coast of Maine without some good vino."

He went to the kitchen and opened the Pinot Noir with a small corkscrew he always carried in his day backpack—just for moments like this. He opened the bottle carefully and set it on the counter to breathe. Looking in an overhead cabinet, he was pleased to find two small wine glasses and, while mentally thanking the court owners for such foresight, cleaned one of them. He then poured himself about a half glass of the fragrant Pinot and let that set for a moment as well. Finally, he took a nice drink of the wine, swirled it around in his mouth and let it slowly slide down his throat.

"Most excellent." He reloaded the glass to nearly three-quarters full. "Time to get to work."

———————————

HE WOKE EARLY THE FOLLOWING morning, before daylight, but felt rested and relaxed. Lying there in the little cabin bed, he congratulated himself on picking such a great place to write. No internet access, no phone calls. Just right for work. He had only begun his new story, not much more than a decently detailed outline and a few opening paragraphs, but it felt like it might develop into something with some size and depth.

Art would imitate an imagined reality, he told himself. The protagonist was a budding author, Leonard Denman, a man not unlike himself. Leonard would travel to some exotic locales and meet Erin Beloit, a beautiful woman of means. They would become involved, physically and emotionally, with a searing, almost frightening passion. And the deeper the relationship became, the more Leonard realized that Erin was herself frightening, physically and emotionally. The affair, explosive to begin, would explode even worse upon its ending. There was danger here—real danger, destructive and life-threatening. That's a good start, he told himself, then rolled over on his side and let himself drift back to sleep.

Around seven thirty, when it was so light inside and out that he was unable to prolong his luxuriant sleep further, he got up and took a walk around the little travel court and then spent the rest of the morning sketching out his story and typing in a few paragraphs of its beginning. Lunch was a PB and J sandwich and by one o'clock he was driving back into Bar Harbor to give the place a more thorough checking out.

On his way into town, he saw a sign for Hull Cove and Acadia National Park, so he turned off there and found their visitor center. Inside, he got a map of the park with directions to trails going up Mt. Cadillac. Driving on, he found a nice secluded trailhead and, leaving the car parked nearby, set off to see the mountain.

The trail was quite wooded at first, thick with brush and small trees, but it was cool and shady and climbed gradually so that it was a pleasant walk more than a strenuous hike. In a short time, the trail rose a bit more steadily and soon he came out of the woods and onto the rocky, grassy slopes leading up to the top of the mountain. Out in the sunlight, it was warmer and he breathed in the clean, coastal air. The sky was almost empty of clouds and was a deep, deep blue.

About mid-way up the mountain, he stopped and stood on a flat, gray rock to look back. And there it was. The Atlantic Ocean. Blue and blue and more blue as far as the eye could see. To the horizon. The blue was lit up with occasional flashes of bright sunlight dancing across the tranquil sea in shimmering yellow patches. He took in a long, deep breath and sighed. It was an extraordinary place, a magnificent view. He stood there several minutes more admiring the sea and then headed back up the hill.

Maybe three-quarters of the way to the top he found another big gray rock, this one large enough and prominent enough to actually sit down on. Tossing his day bag down on the rock, he turned again toward the sea. Unbidden, the memory of a recently lost uncle came to mind. Sitting down by his bag, he used the moment to commune with the sea and to say a personal, inner farewell to his uncle, who had always been one of his favorites. He closed his eyes to the brightness of the shining sea and remained quiet for several moments.

When he felt the goodbye was over he opened his eyes again. Turning to look up the hill, he noticed that there was a parking area at the top and a growing crowd of people there.

"That's good enough," he said. "Good enough for today."

Picking up his bag, he hopped off the big rock and headed back down the trail away from the top of Cadillac Mountain. It would take him a while to get to the car and he was getting hungry. It was time to head into town and check out Bar Harbor some more.

———————

"COULD I JUST HAVE A grilled cheese, French fries, and water?" He said to the waitress.

"Of course, sir. I'll get that in for you and bring the water right away."

"Thanks."

He had ducked into the little café after only a few minutes in town because he was simply too hungry to do a full touristy runaround. The restaurant, Di's Place, seemed like it would be quiet and intimate and it didn't disappoint. For a few moments he sat there quietly sipping the water his waitress brought and thinking about the next section of the story he was working on.

"Just visiting?" A woman's voice from nearby suddenly broke into his literary reverie.

"I'm sorry?" He turned to face a small table just to his right.

"Forgive me," the woman said. "You looked like you might be a tourist."

"Definitely a tourist." He checked the woman out. She appeared to be in her mid to late thirties, unadorned with fine, smooth features. Her soft brown hair fell fashionably to her shoulders and highlighted her softly angular face. "Is it that obvious?"

"The backpack and hiking shoes give you away."

"Don't the locals hike around here?"

"Not usually with airline baggage tickets on their packs."

"Got me there."

"I didn't mean to be rude." She surprised him with a rather familiar wink.

"Oh, no." Lou was intrigued by her attitude. "Are you a local?"

"Here comes your meal." The woman pointed ahead to where Lou's waitress was approaching with a tray of food.

"Yeah, that's some fast service."

"Here you are, sir." The waitress placed the sandwich and fries on the table. "Can I get you anything else?"

"I don't think so." He spotted a bottle of catsup on the table. "I'm all set."

As the waitress walked away, the woman next to Lou also rose.

"I'll leave you to your food." she said pleasantly.

"Well… I'm… uh, Lou Decker."

He reached out his hand. The woman took his hand in hers and held it gently but firmly.

"Erica Bell, pleased to meet you."

"My pleasure."

"Well, have a nice meal, Lou Decker." She turned to go.

"What's good to do here?" he said. "I mean for a tourist and all?"

"Whale watching." She walked away. "Whale watching is always fun."

"Thanks," he said to her retreating figure. "Sounds like a plan."

Erica waved a slender hand as she exited the front of the restaurant. Lou watched her turn right outside and disappear.

Erica Bell, he thought, biting into his grilled cheese and nibbling on a French fry. *Erin Beloit.* That's pretty coincidental. What are the odds of that happening?

———————————

HE GOT UP EARLY THE next morning, despite another relatively late night of wine drinking and writing, and headed back into Bar Harbor. It was easy to find the whale watching boats. The harbor was down at the end of Main Street and you could hardly miss the signs pointing there.

It was another spectacular day, not a cloud to be seen, sunny, with a high, deep blue sky above—perfect for trying to spy the first whale spout as the captain told the eighty or so passengers on the vessel he guided out to sea. The only potential problem Lou saw with the day was that it was on the cool side. He was glad he had picked up the pullover but they were barely away from shore when he realized the sweater was not going to be heavy enough to repel the ocean wind.

From practically the moment the boat got into the open sea, he was watching the horizon for signs of whales. Despite the uncomfortable breeze, he found a space forward on the starboard side of the ship and took up station there. About forty-five minutes out of port, his body shaking from the cold, he saw one of the most amazing sights of his life—the spout of a whale far in the distance, opposite where he stood, to the port side.

"Whale," he cried out excitedly, not knowing whether he should go with 'Thar she blows' or not. "Whale. I see a spout!"

"Well done, sir." A nearby crew member said. "Good spotting. Whale off the port bow."

Lou was thrilled as the captain steered the boat to port, right toward where the spout had appeared. He was about to burst with pride for having seen the first whale. To see better, he crossed over to the forward port side and stood near the railing in hopes of getting a really close up look at the whale.

In fact, when the boat finally reached the whale, he was thrilled anew to see that there were actually three of the giant animals, two large and one smaller one. The captain carefully stayed as near to the whales as he could without disturbing them in order to give the passengers a great view of the creatures.

"I wonder what kind they are?" Lou asked a man to his right.

"I'm not sure," the man said, "but I'm sure they'll tell us in a minute."

"They're Right Whales," a familiar voice to his left said. "They're rare and seldom seen. They're on the endangered species. We're really lucky today."

"Erica? I didn't see you anywhere on the boat before. How…?"

"Wait." She stopped his question with a raised hand. "The crew is about to tell us about the whales."

Over the ship's loudspeaker, a crew member did in fact identify the huge ocean-going mammals as rare Right Whales and based on the similar size of the two larger ones and the presence of the calf, was confident that the bigger animals were both female. He went on to describe the callosities, rough ugly patches of skin on their heads and near their mouths that allowed researchers to identify specific animals. Lou happily soaked in all the new information but was just as impressed by Erica's dead on knowledge. In addition, her sudden appearance had all the hallmarks of a remarkable, and potentially enjoyable, serendipity.

"You nailed that," he told her as the Right Whales began to move away from the boat, out toward less crowded waters.

"But you spotted them."

"You heard that? Saw that?"

"That's how I found you."

"Pretty good luck, I'd say."

"That's one way of looking at it."

On the way back in, they never left each other's side. They stayed by the rail, brisk as the air was, and chatted steadily about the beautiful sea, the magnificent whales, anything that came to mind. He told her he was a writer, in Maine to work on a story. She snuggled next to him as he talked, surprising him with her willingness to be so physical so shortly after meeting him. As if on cue, she linked her arm through his and leaned into him. He had to admit it felt really good to be with her, to feel her warm body next to his out there in the cold air of the deck.

Back in Bar Harbor, with the day of whale watching concluded successfully, they decided to grab a drink and a bite to eat at a bar and grill just down Main Street rather than go their separate ways just yet.

"Something to drink first?" their waitress said.

"Yeah," Lou said, "a Sam Adams, please."

"Yes, sir." The young woman smiled sweetly.

"A beer man?" Erica rolled her eyes dramatically. "Bring me a Chardonnay?"

"Yes, ma'am."

"And don't call me, ma'am, I'm not your mother."

"She was just being polite," Lou said, after the girl had left for the drinks.

"Naturally, being a man, you fell for that." Erica surprised him with her rather rancorous attitude toward the waitress. "She's just working you for a tip."

"Seems a bit harsh."

"Let's not talk about it anymore."

"Right, let's keep the day going well. It was too much fun, too enjoyable, for any minor disagreement. I'll be ready to order something when she gets back for sure. I'm getting hungry."

"I say we have an appetizer and then split something."

"Okay."

She ordered breaded mushrooms for their appetizer and a large hot veggie sandwich to share for the meal. That suited Lou fine and he ordered another beer to go along with the sandwich. She sipped her wine with the food and declined a second glass when the waitress checked on them.

"Well." He patted his full stomach when they had finished the sandwich. "That was tasty. Nice choice."

"I'm glad you liked it." Erica flashed her high voltage smile.

"You must've been here before. You knew exactly what to get, like a local."

"Is that an attempt to figure out who I am, where I come from?"

"Oh, no, no. I just meant…."

"If you're going to get all personal." She again surprised him with her attitude. "Maybe it's time for me to go."

"No, please, I'm sorry. I didn't mean to pry. I was just talking. I didn't mean anything by it."

"Well, it's getting late anyway." She made as if to stand up.

"Wait, just a second. I need to make a pit stop and pay for our food and stuff. I'll walk you to your car, if you have to take off."

Without waiting for a response, he headed for the restroom. When he came out, she was gone. He hurriedly paid for the meal and drinks and over-tipped the waitress to make up for Erica's rudeness. Outside, he looked in both directions but there was no sign of his rather mysterious day's partner. She had vanished into the heart of Bar Harbor somewhere. Gone without a trace. Shaking his head, Lou walked back to the harbor parking and drove his rental car out to the tourist court.

That night, sober and reflective, he wrote up the day's experiences as fiction, describing them just as they had happened but attributing them to the Leonard Denman and Erin Beloit characters in his story. The extraordinary irony and strangeness of the parallels between his personal life and his fictive one were not lost on him. The whole experience was amazing, exhilarating, a little frightening. He knew he would have to pursue it again wherever it might lead.

EARLY NEXT MORNING HE DROVE back into Bar Harbor to spend some time just walking around, absorbing the feel, sound, and smell of the town. He stopped in touristy stores selling all manner of Maine and northeast memorabilia, chatted with salespeople and small business owners, did his best to get a feel for the personality of the place.

Like most towns that profited to a large extent from the tourist trade, Bar Harbor had that atmosphere of the transitory. Each day or so, the population of visitors would change over, leaving the small cadre of business folk to remain and replay the same jokes, friendly smiles, and local stories that they had just told the previous group. Lou had seen it in towns from Show Low, Arizona to Myrtle Beach, South Carolina and beyond.

You, the visitor, were the eternal outsider whose primary function was to provide a living for the townies, whose primary function was to act as if you were the first person to ever truly fit into their world and do so in less than twenty-four hours. Because he understood this symbiotic relationship Lou went along with it and always enjoyed himself and felt comfortable in tourist towns.

Around noon, in a good mood but ready to do something other than check out any more shops, he decided to find a place to have a drink and maybe a snack or meal of some kind. Without really paying attention, he found a little eatery and walked in.

He immediately realized he had gone back to Di's Place, where he first met Erica. And sure enough there she was again, sitting at the same table as the first day. Given their peculiar last parting, he briefly considered turning right back around and leaving but before he could put that idea into action, she looked up and saw him.

"Lou." She enthusiastically rose partway out of her chair.

"Stay seated," he told her.

"Join me, will you? I promise I'll behave."

"Well…."

"Please." Another of her brilliant smiles sealed the deal.

"Sure, why the heck not?"

"I wanted to call you," she said, after he had settled in and placed his food and drink order, "but I didn't know where you were staying and we didn't exchange phone numbers."

"I turned my phone off. I'm trying to get past a small writer's block I've had lately."

"Oh, I didn't realize. I was under the impression your writing was going well."

"It's been going better lately, that is, when people don't just run out and leave me in the lurch."

"I'm sorry I ran away yesterday. I behaved badly, I know."

"It's okay, it actually helped me write later."

"I doubt that."

"No, really," he insisted as his food arrived at the table. "It really did."

"Whatever. I'm glad to see you again."

"Yeah, me, too."

Later, after the meal, they took Lou's car and drove around Acadia National Park. He showed her where he had gone into the park on his hike and then they continued on up to the parking lot at the top of Cadillac Mountain. The afternoon was cool but bright and sunny, just like the previous days he had been in Bar Harbor.

They got out and walked, arms around each other's waists, across the parking lot and out onto the large gray rocks that dotted the side of Cadillac Mountain all the way down to where the woods started at the bottom of the hill. And spread out to the horizon beyond the land was the great, shimmering Atlantic Ocean.

"Majestic, isn't it?" Erica said.

"Totally. Absolutely magnificent."

"Are you glad you came to Bar Harbor?"

"Yes."

"So am I." She kissed him lightly on the cheek.

He pulled her tightly against his side. She slipped a hand into the back pocket of his jeans.

"Nice and tight."

"Likewise I'm sure." He put his left hand on her bottom in response.

"You're a bad boy."

"Always. All the time."

"I'd better be careful, then."

"Maybe you should."

"Maybe I don't want to be careful." She put her arms around his waist and moved up close to his chest.

"Maybe I don't want you to, either." He pulled her against him.

"You're calling the shots."

"You want to come back with me to my little cabin?"

"I'd love to."

On the way back to his place, they stopped off for snacks and a couple of bottles of wine. She continued to surprise him with her seemingly easy acquiescence. It was a side of her that he had not picked up on before nor expected—at least to this point.

After a few glasses of wine, however, that all changed. She again became the aggressor and practically pushed him into bed. She climbed on top, removed both of their clothes. Went after him wildly. It was incredible sex. Athletic, energetic, unrestrained, no holds barred intercourse. It was sex like he imagined it might be with some semi-crazed, totally free woman— rough, steady, pleasurable to the extreme, and with that edge of danger not knowing what might happen next.

Later, exhausted, he lay in bed watching her sleep the sleep of the unconcerned. Her breath was shallow and soft and she seemed completely at ease as she slept. Looking over her near perfect body, a stray thought flitted across his mind. From some place, some odd corner of his mind, it occurred to him that she seemed not quite real lying there so peacefully. Who was she? Could this be real? Was it really happening to him?

With a sigh, he laid his head on the pillow, and put his arms up around the back of his head. He thought of his story, waiting for him there in the laptop, waiting for him to bring it to life again. To make something out of nothing, to convert experience and idea into literature.

As he closed his eyes and drifted toward sleep, he wondered if in fact he was on the right track with his work. Was he marshaling creativity and reality into a dramatic whole, or was he in fact simply blurring the fine distinction that existed between the actual world and fiction? Maybe it didn't matter. Maybe it was the only thing that did.

———————

WHEN HE OPENED HIS EYES next, the morning sun had penetrated the cabin in long yellow fingers of light. Squinting against the brightness, he turned over to find Erica gone.

He slid from the bed to an upright position—maybe a little too quickly. "Ooh." He grabbed his head and sat back down on the edge of the bed. When the pain subsided, he stood up again, but much more slowly. "Erica?"

He realized, then, given the size of the little cabin, that there was no way she was still there. He wasn't sure he was as bothered by that fact as he would have expected himself to be. In the short time she'd been part of his life, her behavior, while highly stimulating on several levels, had been rather erratic to say the least. But there was something about her, besides her intrinsic beauty, that intrigued him, made him want to be in her presence even if that meant dealing with the complexities of her nature.

Reluctantly he accepted the fact that she had gone for the moment and that he would have to go in search of her again if he wanted them to remain in contact. Downing a tall glass of orange juice to jumpstart his morning and delay his hunger before having breakfast, he found a dry, clean towel and headed for the shower.

He let the water run until it was comfortably hot and then stood there for a good while just letting it warm up his body and ease the pain in his head. He knew he had to go into town and find Erica but he would take his time. He was sure he knew how to find her. She hadn't made it all that difficult so far.

———————————

HE DECIDED NOT TO DRIVE into town until around ten-thirty. He didn't want to seem overanxious or eager, which he assumed would get him nowhere with Erica. Even though he still had a bit of a hangover after cleaning up and eating and was not particularly inspired to write, he still managed to work a little bit on his manuscript before heading into Bar Harbor. All the way in, he had this nagging sensation that the story was getting away from him, that his real-life involvement with Erica was finding its way into his fiction—altering and informing it in a way he had not intended.

Despite his confidence that he would be able to locate her easily and quickly in town, she in fact turned out to be a rather more elusive quarry than he had expected. He tried Di's Place, down by the whale watching harbor, along the rows of tourist shops—nothing. It was altogether possible, he reasoned, that she had simply disappeared, gone back to where she came from—wherever that might be.

He was considering returning to the cabin when an idea flitted across his mind. Cadillac Mountain. It was just a hunch, but how could he go wrong whether she was there or not. There were few places he'd seen with such an inspiring view. At least returning to its summit might provide him with more psychic energy for writing.

By the time he reached the parking lot at the top of the mountain, it was pushing noon and the sun was high and bright. The blue bay beyond shimmered and sparkled, ephemeral patches of gold dancing upon the still water. He parked the car and climbed out to get a better view of the land and sea. Stepping onto one of the ubiquitous gray flat rocks, he took a long, slow look around the area. Just to his left, not more than twenty yards away, he saw her. After a moment, she turned and saw him.

"Are you stalking me?"

"Well—no." He looked around to see if anyone else at the top might be watching or listening to them.

"Could fool me."

"What are you talking about?" He walked over to her. She gave him a haughty look.

"You're going to tell me you're not pursuing me?"

"I was looking for you, sure. I don't know if that's the same as pursuing. You did just sort of disappear on me this morning."

"You were asleep. I left."

"How did you get here?"

"And that is your business, how?"

"Never mind."

"I got a ride with a friend, if you must know."

"Is he, or she, still here?" He looked around.

"It took you long enough to find me. I thought after last night you would be a little more attentive."

"I … I don't know what to say to that."

"Oh, you big dummy." She put her arms around his waist. "You just don't get it, do you?"

"I'm completely confused. I don't even know what I'm supposed to get."

"Of course you don't, silly, that's what I'm for."

"If you say so."

"I'm hungry," she announced. He gave her a questioning look. "You know, food. That stuff that keeps us going, allows us to work and get things done?"

"All right, whatever."

"You have your car?"

"I do."

"Then take me into town and buy me lunch."

"I'm at your service."

"Of course you are. That's how this thing works."

———————

AFTER A QUIET LUNCH, HE drove them back to his cabin where they repeated the previous night's sexual athletics. This time, however, they didn't bother to have even a half glass of wine as a psychic warm up. What they shared this day was straightforward, unadulterated, and highly exhilarating —at least for him. But when it was over, she seemed uneasy, agitated, unable to lie still.

"Are you okay?" He sprawled on top of the bed covers.

"I'm fine." She hopped out of bed and began putting her clothes back on. He watched her silently. "What?"

"Nothing."

"No, you were about to say something. What was it?"

"No I wasn't. I wasn't going to say anything."

There was an icy silence while she finished dressing. He began putting on his clothes as well.

She broke the quiet spell. "You're using me. You're turning our passion into a story. You don't give a damn about me. You just want to use me to create your lousy fiction."

"What are you talking about?"

"Don't try to BS me. I saw your story."

"You were on my laptop? When? This morning while I was asleep?"

"Don't try to avoid your responsibility. You can't get off that easy."

"What the hell is the matter with you? I don't understand what you are talking about?"

"Liar," she said bluntly. "You know exactly what I'm talking about. Hell, you're putting everything I say in your damned story. All you want me for is more material for your story. Admit it."

"It's not like that at all. I swear."

"You writers are all the same. You don't care about anybody or anything unless you can use it in your work."

"I'm not that way."

"Please." She said.

"I promise, and I'll prove it." He reached out for her but she pulled away. "Don't."

"I need you, you have to know that."

"I know what you want from me." She walked to the cabin door. "You always want it."

"Wait…."

But she was quickly gone, shutting the door behind her. Gone. As simply as that.

He stood still for several moments staring at the closed door. He didn't know if she was really gone or not. Sometimes he wondered if she really existed, despite their intense physical relationship. It was all so strong, so sudden and so fast, he doubted its reality.

"Oh, hell." He slumped down in the little desk chair.

He lifted the cover on his laptop and hit the power button. The system booted up in less than a minute. As soon as he could open MS Word he was back working on his story. Erica be damned.

———————

IN THE CLEAR LIGHT OF the following morning, after a refreshing shower and a light breakfast, he was in a more conciliatory frame of mind. Erica had her points about their relationship. He did tend to use his own experience and his observations about life as the basis for writing, but he wasn't cold and calculating about it.

He lived his relationships, his successes and failures, his hopes, his conflicts, his loves. It was just that as a writer, all of it was fair game to be turned into fiction. That was what a writer did, was. He still cared about people, places, life but he had to maintain a distance from them—authorial distance. It wasn't an easy thing, but it came with the territory.

Mid-morning he went into town in search of her yet again. Instinctively, he headed toward Di's Place. He found a parking spot about a block away from the restaurant and walked slowly and calmly toward it. Just as he was about to jaywalk across the narrow street to Di's, he saw her. She was coming up the sidewalk—arm-in-arm with another man. He froze where he was.

Neither she nor her new beau were paying any attention to their surroundings. They were completely into each other. She had her arm through his and they were smiling and laughing as if they'd known each other for years. Lou sized the guy up quickly. Another writer, he thought, or an artist. One looking for that shot of inspiration or a muse that would provide the wind through his metaphorical Aeolian Harp.

It was all so familiar to Lou that the anger initially welling up in him simply dissipated into the air of the new reality. He understood her throwing him over, understood how this worked. The man she was with was today's best catch just as he had been the best catch each of the last few days. That's how life was—you were the latest and greatest and then you were yesterday's news.

He started to turn around and head back to the car but stopped when he saw her look in his direction. He wished he had kept going for she looked right at him, through him. It was like they had never known each other at all. Like it had all been a dream, or in his imagination.

She and the younger guy went through the door into Di's place and disappeared. Was that how it always worked with her, he wondered? Did she just pop up in your life, in your mind maybe, and then when she had used you—or you had used her—it was all over?

Over. Definitely over. He certainly knew that now. But he still felt that odd mix of sensations when he finished a story, a poem, a book—elation tempered by a feeling of emptiness. A hole where the energy and drive had been. The way probably everyone felt when they reached a goal or completed a difficult task. It was great while it was happening but when it was over there was that ambiguous sense of pleasure mixed with a feeling of hollowness.

He took a deep breath and exhaled loudly. That was all there was to it. It had come and gone. He had his moment and now it was time to move on. He turned away from Di's Place and walked to the rental car. On the way back to the cabin, he picked up a really good bottle of wine and some tasty treats.

He would finish his story tonight. It would be done and he would move on from Erica Bell. He would complete the story of Erin Beloit and Leonard Denman and maybe that would give him some distance from himself as well as satisfy the New York literary people. Workers in fiction were rare birds and he himself was perhaps a rare one among them. Who knew? It was just what you did.

The following morning, sober and maybe a little bit humbler, he packed up his laptop and bags and drove back down the coast. He already had a new idea for a completely different kind of story. He thought Charlie, his agent, might approve of it even though it didn't involve a woman or a relationship.

It would be something not so connected to his own personal experience. He thought he would like to do a story like that. It wouldn't be nearly so hard, so dangerous to write as the personal kind. Yeah, he could definitely write something born of his imagination. He might even be able to make it into another book. He knew his publishers would like that.

J.B. HOGAN is a prolific and award-winning author. He grew up in Fayetteville, Arkansas, but moved to Southern California in 1961 before entering the U. S. Air Force in 1964. After the military, he went back to college, receiving a Ph.D. in English from Arizona State University in 1979.

J.B. has published over 250 stories and poems. His novels, *The Apostate, Living Behind Time, Losing Cotton,* and *Tin Hollow*—as well as his local baseball history book, *Angels in the Ozarks,* a short story collection entitled *Fallen,* and his book of poetry, *The Rubicon*—are available at Amazon, iBooks, Barnes & Noble, Books-A-Million, and Walmart.

When he's not writing or teaching, J.B. plays upright bass in East of Zion, a family band specializing in bluegrass-flavored Americana music, and is active in the Washington County (AR) Historical Society, where he serves on the board as as a Past President.

www.thejbhogan.com

CPSIA information can be obtained
at www.ICGtesting.com
Printed in the USA
BVHW041722241022
650027BV00001B/36